The Gene Gun

James A. Cunningham, Ph.D.

Copyright

Publisher

*Front cover illustration is original artwork done
by James A. Cunningham and Iveta Trifonova*

The Gene Gun

A dedicated geneticist on planet Theon sends an android to Earth with 500 dominant gene modifying injections designed to reduce the aggressive nature of Homo sapiens. This effort was viewed by many scholars as the number one critical program toward preventing an all-life-extinguishing nuclear war. Later, in a meeting with the President of United States, the android and his 14 colleagues are placed under arrest, triggering a high-tech counterattack by the androids.

James A. Cunningham, Ph.D.

Some people would think that a man who is 88 years old and has had Parkinson's disease for the past seven years would not be able to write. This would be true. But he might be able to type.

The author James A. Cunningham, seen above at age 73, earned a PhD from the University of Texas in 1961. He then worked 47 years in the field of semiconductor devices and integrated circuits for several corporations and then as an a consultant. He has generated 47 U.S. patents in electronic devices, and published 17 technical papers. He has lived in Silicon Valley, California since 1972.

"*All wars are boyish, and are fought by boys.*"
-Herman Melville, 1866

Contents

Preface

Aggression

This is a work of fiction. Thus, some of the action and events presented within are driven by capabilities and inventions not yet realized. This, of course, is not an unusual aspect in works of fiction written by Homo sapiens. However, the author contends that the primary driving force for the story presented here involves a common concern in all societies where the human species Homo sapiens are in control. The problem is not actually fictional, but is a widely supported belief by archeologists and others that we, Homo sapiens, are fundamentally so aggressive and lacking in empathy that in time we will destroy ourselves and perhaps all life in a horrendous all-out nuclear war and planet wide conflagration.

Many hundreds of thousands of years ago a human-like species fought and struggled for survival and aggression provided certain benefits as it does even today.

Certain results suggest that a favorable perception of violence may be a useful adaption to insecure and violent living conditions reducing the vulnerability of children for trauma-related mental disorders.

And of course aggressive behaviors would likely result in advantages in biological evolution since it has some benefits for the survival of species

In terms of acceptance, tolerance, and empathy between various groups of people, many of us humans remain ambivalent. But some of us remain strongly prejudicial toward certain groups. They remind us of the old adage, 'birds of a feather flock together'.

Others revere tolerance and view such positions as nonsensical, insisting that people can and should be evaluated on an individual basis. In support of that view, we can find many examples of different people living happily close together in their own separate neighborhoods. In San Francisco we find a large area called Chinatown. New York City has its Harlem.

On the other hand are several examples, below, where racial or ethnic prejudice still appear.

2014–2015

City of Atlanta: 45% White
Percentage in white neighborhood: 57%

City of Detroit: 22% Black
Percentage in Black neighborhood: 69%

City of Los Angeles: 45% Hispanic
Percentage in Hispanic neighborhood: 63%

The above data shows that some level of prejudice still exists in the US. But it does not prove that it is a problem. So what is the origin or basis for many scholars who insist that Homo sapiens are dangerously aggressive?

We can readily cite many archeologists who believe that Homo sapiens are an aggressive species. Their position arises mainly from two areas: (1) our violent evolutionary past and (2) our continued engagements in wars and our never-ending massive preparations for new wars. Anthropologists also insist that even though we may have various skin colors, different physical features, vastly different values, unequal IQs, widely varying physical capabilities and various levels of success, we humans are nevertheless now all of one race—Homo sapiens.

And most of us have also heard that when we humans began evolving perhaps half a million years ago that at least nine other human-like species were also present, all competing for survival. Some of these human-like beings bear still familiar names such as Neanderthals, the very early Australopithecus. So, where are they?

Most scientists who study such things believe that with our superior tool and weapon making skills, we Homo sapiens killed them all.

The following analysis of the emergence of dominant species Homo sapiens is mainly a condensed and lightly edited version of the publication, "Nine Species of Human Once Walked Earth. Now There's Just One. Did We Kill The Rest?" by Nick Longrich, *The Conversation,* 22 November 2019.

There is no evidence to distinguish between any of the early human-like species in terms of their ability to think and to analyze their environments. That we are the only species to survive is not convincing evidence of our greater intelligence. Known human history shows intense aggression and continuing genocide. One of the last surviving human species who lived with us back in time, species Homo neanderthals, were stocky hunters adapted to Europe's cold regions. The more primitive Homo erectus lived there as well. Several short, small-brained species also survived there for some time. One species of an archaic human was discovered in 2013 in a South African cave dated to the Middle Pleistocene or 335,000–236,000 years ago. Homo luzonensis lived in the Philippines. Homo floresiensis could be found in Indonesia. However, by 10,000 years ago, they were all gone. The disappearance of these species resembles a mass extinction. But there was no obvious environmental catastrophe, volcanic eruption, climate change, or asteroid impact driving it. Instead, the extinctions' timing suggests they were caused by the spread of a new species, evolving 260,000–350,000 years ago in Southern Africa. Guess who? Homo sapiens.

The spread of modern humans out of Africa caused a sixth mass extinction, an event greater than the 40,000-year event extending from the disappearance of Ice Age mammals to the destruction of rain forest today.

Many workers in this field believe we are a uniquely dangerous species. We hunted wooly mammoths, ground sloths and other large mammals to extinction.

We have destroyed plains and forests for farming, modifying over half the planet's land area. We have altered the planet's climate.

We are even dangerous to other human populations because we compete for resources and land. History is full of examples of people warring, displacing and wiping out other groups over territory; from Rome's destruction of Carthage, to the American conquest of the West and the British colonization of Australia. Lacking empathy even for our own kind, we have seen genocides and ethnic cleansing in Bosnia, Rwanda, Iraq, Darfur and Myanmar.

Like language or tool use, a capacity for and tendency to engage in genocide is arguably an instinctive part of human nature. There's little reason to think that early Homo sapiens were less territorial, less violent, less intolerant—less human.

Optimists have sometimes painted early hunter-gatherers as peaceful, noble savages, and have argued that our culture, not our nature, creates violence. But field studies, historical accounts, and archaeology all show that war in primitive cultures was intense, pervasive and lethal.

Neolithic weapons such as clubs, spears, axes and bows, combined with guerrilla tactics like raids and ambushes, were devastatingly effective. Violence was the leading cause of death among men in these societies, and wars saw higher casualty levels per person than World Wars I and II.

Complex tools and culture would also have helped us efficiently harvest a wider range of animals and plants, feeding larger tribes and giving our species a strategic advantage. However, cooperation, planning, strategies, manipulation and deceit may have been our ultimate weapons.

The incompleteness of the fossil record makes it hard to test these ideas. But in Europe, the only place with a relatively complete archaeological record, fossils show that within a few thousand years of our arrival, Neanderthals vanished.

DNA tells of other encounters with archaic humans. East Asian, Polynesian and Australian groups have DNA from Denisovans. The fact that we interbred with these other species proves that they disappeared only after encountering us.

But why would our ancestors wipe out their relatives, causing a mass extinction—or, perhaps more accurately, a mass genocide?

The answer lies in population growth. Humans reproduce exponentially, like all species. Unchecked, we historically doubled our numbers every 25 years. And once humans became cooperative hunters, we had no predators. Populations grew to exploit the available resources.

Further growth, or food shortages caused by drought, harsh winters or overharvesting resources would inevitably lead tribes into conflict over food and foraging territory. Warfare became a check on population growth, perhaps the most important one.

Our elimination of other species probably wasn't a planned, coordinated effort of the sort practiced by civilizations, but a war of attrition. The end result, however, was just as final. Raid by raid, ambush by ambush, valley by valley, modern humans would have worn down their enemies and taken their land.

Chapter One

Snatching Children in Rome

This is a tale about the people of three planets: Earth, Theon and Fantheon. Earth and Theon each cycled around a star in the usual manner, and both had very similar animal and plant life. Both had evolved with Homo sapiens finally in charge. The differences lay in how long each planet had been developing their knowledge of science and technology. Theon led Earth by 200 years. But Fantheon led the other two by a colossal one million years. On Earth, a million years ago, we had barely evolved to the first Neanderthals. On Fantheon one million years ago they were developing their first androids and spacecraft.

There were still many citizens on planet Fantheon that were of human origin, although because no one aged anymore, their total number was a bit on the wane. Some enjoyed spending a few years occasionally on nearby planets Earth or Theon, although they had to be very careful to not be injured, since their recovery often required special procedures. Another consideration was that the people of Earth were unaware of a planet called Fantheon, while those on Theon viewed the population of Fantheon as rich and charitable.

From time to time Fantheon would send an android to one of the two planets. Their medical people would pick up—or more precisely—abscond, with young people or children from Earth or Theon in order to continue perfecting their long-term travel technology. A trip to one of these planets and back to pick up a child and then return him or her back home could take up to 750 years. During the long trip they could hone their skills of knowledge and language implants, long term stasis, and zero aging. They realized, of course, the basic cruelty of such a thing so they at least compensated the victims monetarily when they woke up 750 years later on their home planet.

Just Outside of Rome, Italy The year 970

Our story opens just outside Rome in a small farm house in the Italian countryside.

"Wake up, my sweet Anna. Remember we are going to Rome today," said Alice Belione. "It's your birthday. You are going to be nine years old. Remember? We are going to your birthday party at Uncle Vittorio's house."

"Will Emma be there?" asked Anna.

"Of course she will and I bet she will have a present for you.".

The mother and daughter had breakfast and left the house at 10:00 am. By 11:30 they had walked the five miles to the city limits of Rome.

"Honey, there is something here in Rome that would be wonderful for you to see before we get to your uncle's house. It is called the Pantheon. It is one of the most beautiful buildings the world and it's not too far from here."

"Let's go," said Anna. Twenty minutes later they were standing before the great structure.

A certain Mr. Cobalt happened to be there as well. Trying to not draw attention to himself, he had dressed in an off-white coverall like a house painter might wear. But a six foot, three inch man who weighs 436 pounds cannot be invisible. If you were close by, you'd feel strange vibrations of energy emanating from him. This particular Model ZQRr4 android from Fantheon was made of steel, ball bearings, cables, silver and copper wire, 65 motors, high speed digital and analog computers, titanium, magnets, proximity devices, sensors, hydraulics, listening devices, communication systems, function generation systems, a large plutonium power supply, various crystals, 50 TB memory, transducers, communication systems and high energy weapons.

He noticed a little girl who was probably nine or ten years old, with her mother. Cobalt gradually moved toward them. He quickly bent over and placed his hands around her chest, lifted her over his head and dropped her into a canvas bag on his upper back. By the time Anna screamed "MOMMEEeeeeeee" , he had reached the street running along the left side of the Pantheon. It happened so fast that by the time Alice Belione screamed, "STOP HIM! STOP HIM!" Mr. Cobalt, running at 60 miles per hour, had already turned down the next street. Then he raced down a wide boulevard, leaving town, passing horses and wagons at 80 miles per hour. He next turned into a wooded area where he had hidden the Flyer. Within 3.5 minutes of leaving the Pantheon he had reached the Flyer. On the way he had injected Anna with a sleep-inducing drug. Anna was in the bag, asleep. Within another two minutes, the Flyer had taken off without a sound.

The journey to Fantheon, some 15 light years away, takes 375 years. During the long first leg of the journey, several changes and improvements would be applied to Anna, including an anti-aging process. During this treatment some aging would occur, usually about 25 years. Thus, when Anna arrived home again she would actually be—and look like—she was 34 years old. She would remember nothing about the journey in the Flyer either during or after the journey. Even when she was studied and examined by doctors upon reaching Fantheon no memories would be found or recorded. One minute she was nine years old, bouncing around in a bag on the back of a running robot, and the next minute, she was at an ocean front harbor, sitting on some grass, seemingly in another and much older person's body.

Chapter Two

Landing in Theon

The Year 1720

The only thing the least bit comforting during the first several minutes after her wake up was when a nice man had come up and asked Anna if she was okay. She had said, "I think so. But where am I?"

He had said "You are on Theon." *Not Rome?* Then she was told the date was not 970. It was now 1720.

Anna thought her mind was about to explode. *Theon? What is Theon?* Then he said something about Capital City. Then little Anna was told that her name was no longer Anna. Her name was now Mother Nature. *What was that again? MOTHER NATURE?* These were her new first and last names.

Then the man took her hand and her luggage and walked over to a nearby picnic area where there were benches, tables and more grass. He then said "Don't worry. I'll be right back...have a quick errand to take care of." As he walked away she told him to be sure to bring her mommy back with him.

On the same day of the abduction of Anna, a nine year-old boy was taken by Mr. Zinc. After the same 700-year process, he was told his name was no longer

Lorenzo Romano. His name would now be one word: Atlas. *What was that again?* ATLAS.

Similar Planets 17 years later
The Year 1737

Imagine finding yourself strolling along the sidewalk in a pleasant upscale neighborhood of quiet streets and large homes set back on grassy lawns. The year is 1737. The streets are all paved and defined by concrete curbs. Puzzled, you notice large openings just about every block at the sides of the streets under the curbs. You hear water trickling down under there somewhere. You see glass globes up on high poles. *Glass globes?* On Earth electric street lights didn't exist in 1737. *What is all this odd stuff? Where is this place?* So many houses. They all have a concrete ramp from the street leading to what appear to be large doors. *What would that be for?* No one has a driveway in a neighborhood like this. There are no cars. And then the most amazing thing of all happens. A sleek looking machine is moving down the street at an amazing rate of speed. You see people inside through glass windows.

Eventually you understand why many things are so different and startling. You are told you are not on planet Earth. You are on Theon, a planet in another star system. Specifically, you are in Capital City, the location of Theon's world government. Then you discover that Theon is as much as 200 years ahead of Earth in science and technology. In many areas, Theon, to you, would look more like 1937 than 1737.

But were years counted the same way on both planets? Theon was persuaded years ago, by a remarkable and influential person we will introduce shortly, to count years in the same way that we do on Planet Earth. This would help in making accurate comparisons between Theon and Earth. For both planets, one day was one planet rotation and one year still took 365 days to make one trip around their star or sun, as in the case of Earth. Small differences forced Theon to make corrections (fractions of a second) on January first each year. Being quite small, the corrections were and still are ignored.

Now focusing on more natural differences, you realize that you have never seen trees like these. The leaves are oddly shaped and some have a slight bluish tint. The shrubs appear unique and cannot be identified. You see two moons in the sky. Finally, you notice a very large house on perhaps four acres with extensive and complex gardens toward the back. You note a large house with a shiny, dark grey titanium metal roof, an unusual feature sometimes mentioned by the general public.

You observe an attractive woman in her thirties strolling around with an athletic, handsome man of probably around the same age. They appear to be checking out the property and the landscaping, touching the leaves and inspecting any new growth over the lush grounds.

The man has a distinctly intelligent look to his face. The couple are deep in conversation as they walk the grounds of the property and observe the landscaping. Eventually you learn that this apparently young and lovely woman is now perhaps a thousand years old. Many accept this as true, but there are still some skeptics. Her real name was buried long ago and everyone now knows her by her somewhat grandiloquent title—Mother Nature. She insisted she once had an identical sister who lived on planet Earth but this sibling perished some time ago in a nitroglycerin explosion. She has an intense interest in Planet Earth. However, in contrast, Earth has no knowledge whatsoever of Theon.

The couple appear still deep in conversation as they walk the grounds of the property.

Mother Nature's male friend's name was Atlas. He lived with her in the house in a separate bedroom. She said he also does not age, and had the quickest mind in the Universe, especially when it comes to numbers and mathematics. If you were to ask Atlas why the planets look so similar even though they are 200 years apart, he would say it is simply because the pace of new technology had moved faster on Theon than on Earth by perhaps 200 years since they both began counting 2,000 years ago.

From time to time Atlas accepted highly complex consulting work from the Theon government.

Those who know him said his sexual parts do not always function properly which explained why he was sometimes in a crabby mood.

The pair had no special powers, other than being far above average in intelligence and the remarkable fact that they simply did not noticeably age. A fact they could not or would not explain.

Both were well known and highly revered around the world of Theon. Mother Nature had repeatedly developed new hybridized grains and other plants that had brought an abundance of food to a growing population. In more recent years, she had focused on gene editing and had helped, via consulting, in successfully eliminating several diseases. For the past four years she had run a fully equipped laboratory in her large home, with four scientists working there full time on gene editing technology.

The date is 1737

Both Mother Nature and Atlas were on their stone paved patio, relaxing in lawn chairs. Atlas looked over toward his companion and said, "My lovely Miss Nature, I have a theory. I think I can explain everything. Why we don't age. Why we have large time gaps in our memories. And why both you and I share the same mysteries in our past."

She replied, "You must be kidding. We have never been able make a dent in that whole mystery. I remember you–"

Interrupting, Atlas said, "First I have a question. Did you tell me maybe ten years ago, that when you were around nine or ten years old you seemed to remember visiting a magnificent building with your mother, and it seemed like for some reason, which still is not clear, that you were on Earth in a city called Rome?"

"Yes, that is true. But on planet Earth? There is no way to get there. How long would it take to travel to Earth? I still remember trying to figure that out. The instruments we launched in our unmanned space probes that we have been sending to explore the other planets in our star system can reach a top speed of about 40,000 miles per hour. If we had a spacecraft that could move that fast—which we don't—it would take 800 years to travel from Theon to Earth. And another 800 to get back. And I recall that came to about 20 tons per person. That's impossible. You would also have to bring enough food, water and oxygen for it to happen. Traveling to Fantheon from Earth would take over 22,000 years."

"I absolutely agree, my dear. It would never happen that way. But what about our new Mr. Steel the android? Our man Steel is about to take your gene editing process to Earth, right? And it will take 100 years of travel in the space Flyer from here. It will take 20 tons of food. Didn't I hear you say this morning that he is leaving tomorrow?"

"Yes that's right, but Steel doesn't eat, drink, breathe, wash or use a bathroom. He won't even get bored. He'll just switch himself off."

"Let's come back to the travel problem in a few minutes. One of the more famous buildings on Earth was constructed and opened in the year 125. This is the Pantheon in Rome." Atlas placed several photographs of the building on a coffee table next to the lady.

Mother Nature looked and gasped, "My God, that is it! But how could that be? There is no way I could have been on Earth. This makes no sense."

"I will tell you in just a few minutes. But first, please tell me, when did your big memory loss begin? Isn't that where the gap in time begins? After seeing buildings in Rome?"

"Yes, the next thing I remember, I was sitting on some grass in the harbor of Capital City, just a few miles from here. It was an awful feeling—bizarre, scary, impossible. I didn't know who I was. Even my childhood memories were gone. But wait. I have never told anyone my story. It's a tale from a crazy person. Perhaps I should keep this to myself."

"Come now, you know you are safe with me You know I love you. You know we would be married if not for my sex problem.

"Could be. But you told me some years ago that I might be your sister? Not that it would be a big problem, but I know enough about genetics to say that would not be possible. But okay. I do trust you, of course. So, let me continue…There I was, just awakened, sitting on some grass, not knowing what to do next. A nice looking older man in a dark suit walked up and said 'Good morning, my name is Robert Nation. Are you Mother Nature?' I answered, 'Mother Nature? Well, in this bag I was just looking through that's what it says on some papers. Is that who you are looking for?' I suddenly realized that I could read. The words made sense!"

"I asked him if my mommy was with him. He ignored the question. Before Nation arrived, I had awakened on a grass lawn near the ocean and saw nothing that looked familiar. I looked at my body. It couldn't be...I was a full-grown woman! The day before I had been nine years old. Now how old was I? I had no idea. I felt like a freak. I noticed a student walking by. I got up off the ground and motioned for him to stop. I began asking him if there was a nearby clinic for…I stopped. Was I speaking gibberish? No. I realized later that I had been speaking normal but highly accented Theonese. But where did it come from? It was impossible. I looked over to the student and said to him 'Scusami tanto' in Italian. Where had that come from? He turned and walked quickly away, glad to be away from the crazy woman. Now I am confusing my confusion!"

"Missy, my sweet Missy, I will tell you exactly where the languages came from, but for now let's continue with what happened that first day. Let's review that day in detail. It's loaded with clues."

"But Italian? How could that be? I went back to my spot on the grass and I was looking into my two pieces of luggage. Ignoring the clothes, I examined the papers: no birth certificate, a high school diploma from a foreign country, and a BS degree in Biology from a school I'd never heard of. I have never shown anyone these papers."

She stood suddenly and muttered to herself, "Breathe in. Breathe out." Mother Nature appeared agitated.

Atlas then said, "Wait just a minute here. You are getting very upset. We have all the time we need. Let's take a little break. I'll go into the house and get some wine. I will be right back."

A few minutes later Atlas poured a deep red wine into two large crystal glasses and she continued with the story.

"Robert Nation returned. He said, 'Hello again, Miss Nature. I was instructed by the mayor of Capital City to pick you up and take you to your new home. Sorry about being a little late. Had to stop and get gas for the car.' I said, 'Gas? Car? What are you talking about?' He said, 'The mayor said you have been away a while.' He picked up my two pieces of luggage and we started walking away. 'I don't think I can find the words to describe where I have been. Just tell me what the words 'car' and 'gas' mean,' I requested. 'Okay,' he said and went on about fuel and carriages and piston engines."

"Atlas, I hope you don't mind me telling you all this with the dialogue. I have gone over this so many times in my head. It's like reading a book out loud."

"No problem. You are making it very clear what happened," said Atlas.

"Mr. Nation then explained how cars are made. He said, 'In a few minutes you'll see a car. There are many thousands of them in the city. Another word for car is automobile. Here comes one now! When they were first invented people called them horseless carriages.'"

"Anyway, I glimpsed my first car soon after. We got into his large, comfortable car and ten minutes later we were here, at my place. I saw a nice stone cottage on a big lot. Mr. Nation parked, grabbed my bags and headed for the front door, which opened before we were on the front porch. A woman stepped out and greeted us warmly and announced that she was my housekeeper and cook. She said that her name was Landa. 'Fine with me.' I said, not knowing what else to say. I went into the kitchen and opened the large refrigerator and saw an abundance of food on the sparkling clean glass shelves inside. Landa showed me the large bedroom and bathroom where she opened the tap on a large white bathtub and started taking off my clothes. I was too tired to resist. I recall a warm tub bath that was wonderful. Pretty soon the nice lady was making supper. It was wonderful as well. The next day Mr. Nation dropped by and said we were to meet the mayor in his office the day after tomorrow. I agreed, of course, and we were there about one o'clock in the afternoon."

"So, that afternoon we were both there! I don't really have to review what happened next but I will, just to make sure we are both in agreement. In the room that day, the year was 1720. The Mayor of Capital City, a lawyer named Robert Austin, Mr. Nation, and you, Atlas, who had been staying in one of the bedrooms at the cottage. Robert Austin then gave a rather detailed speech. One I will never forget. The following is close to his exact words: 'I represent a group of very wealthy persons who must remain nameless and absolutely unidentifiable. First they want to apologize for what they have put you through over the past years. We have robbed you of your childhood and modified your brains without your permission. All illegal acts, of course."

"Next let's list and state the changes and additions that were made to your brains and to your bodies. For female person Mother Nature, we have implanted a high-level knowledge of Biology and Genealogy out to the year 2060. We will send updates to you every six months by mail until 2000, that is for the next 280 years. Should you so choose, you could become the most famous genealogist in two worlds. We also implanted the local language. For male person Atlas we implanted a thorough knowledge of mathematics as known up to the year 1950. We placed no constraints on this. Also implanted was the local language. We have made arrangements with the local University of Capital City for you to soon take written tests. Upon passing your tests you will be awarded Ph.D. degrees in your field. We have also insured that both of you will be unaffected by the future passing of time. In other words, you will no longer age. However, you could still die upon injury. We have also arranged for financial compensation. Each of you will receive 500 pounds of gold. The gold has already been placed in the City Bank under your names. Here are credit cards you may use, as of today. Finally, in order to maintain ownership of the gold and avoid a lawsuit, you must agree that you will not pursue or make any effort to identify persons who are or might be responsible for the gold or the knowledge implants, or changes in your rates of aging. Should that happen the gold ownership will immediately disappear and you will be the subject of a lawsuit. The land upon which the cottage stands, which is 4.5 acres, and the cottage itself is already owned by

Miss Nature. The housekeeper and cook, Miss Landa, has been paid up for two years.' …An hour later we both signed the document." she concluded.

"Excellent presentation, my dear. You even remembered exactly what the people said! Very impressive. Do you recall that on the way out of the mayor's office a big guy came up and said he was the man with me when I arrived back here? I think I told him that he seemed vaguely familiar. 'Look me up at the cottage tomorrow,' I told him and Nation gave him directions."

"I remember him. He gave me the creeps," said Mother Nature.

"I am not surprised. His name is Mr. Indium, an android. And, well, I sort of got him a job in the Physics department. The physics guys were quite impressed by him. I still see him occasionally. A few days ago, I was asking him about the Flyers. He said they travel in space at a maximum of 4% of the speed of light. He reminded me that he had been with me on the second half of the journey. With that, I now know what happened when we were taken from Rome," said Atlas.

"Atlas, this better be good. I don't think I can stand reviewing this again."

"No problem. Just listen." said Atlas. "Let's take a close look at planet Fantheon. Firstly, consider they are said to be a million years ahead of us in science and technology. Consider also that we on Theon are only at most 300 to 400 years from the start of the industrial age. Only 400 years ago we had no radios, no TV, no automobiles, no aircraft and no telephones. We had no electric power, no plastic, no sources of light except fire, no stainless steel, no electric motors, no movies, no factories, no freeways, no air conditioners, no photography, no electric fans, no trains and so on."

"It is hard to imagine what one million years of research and industrial development would bring. Fantheon probably has had Steel type androids for the past 100,000 years. The number of flesh and blood people in their society—assuming there are still some there, which is unknown—might be sending men like Steel to pick up ordinary people to determine how well their new technologies are working. Maybe they wanted to travel in space themselves? In order to do that they would need (1) a method for placing a person in full stasis for as long as needed, (2) a technology of stopping the process of aging and (3) a method of transferring knowledge, such as one or more of the sciences and languages. You and I, my dear, received all three."

"We were both fluent upon arrival, in the language used in this part of planet Theon. We also knew Italian. The journey in the Flyer requires two androids. So the trip was not from Rome to here. It had to be from Rome to Fantheon, and finally to here. The time for the Flyer to travel 15 light years at 4% the speed of light is 375 years. Two times that is 750 years."

"We now know your birth year. We arrived here in 1720. Subtracting 750 and 9 yields 961. I would guess we lost about 25 years during the flights. That would make you about 9 plus 25, so 34 years old in physical years. From your birth date in 961 to 2020 for example, you will be 1059 years old."

"Atlas, I must admit your analysis is convincing. But doing this implant without anyone's permission is grossly unethical! I will never know what my real name is or know who my parents were," said Mother Nature.

"You are right about the ethics. Power corrupts. But you might be able to recover some of your childhood memories. I have picked up some. My real name is Lorenzo Romano. I was living in Rome. I remember the son of a bitch who snatched me off the sidewalk. But, I like the name Atlas. I like math. It could be worse," said Atlas.

"Laughing, Mother Nature replied, "Atlas, that is wonderful. I have underestimated you…I understand you saw the math professor at the University. How did that go?"

"I did call him. It went well. Maybe too well. His name is Dr. Neighbors, and he knew all about the test and the Ph.D. deal. I asked him if I could meet him that day. He agreed to meet me. I had Nation take me to his building, He was sitting in his office when I went in and introduced myself. He was very friendly. I liked the guy immediately. After a few minutes I told him that if he already had it ready, I would like to take the test right then. He agreed, so I went into a conference and worked on the test. It took about 40 minutes. Without the math implant I would have flunked it. He looked it over and said he had never seen anyone finish one of those tests that fast. He read my answers and said they were all correct. He offered me a position on the math staff. I told him I would be honored to join his staff, but asked for a few days to settle in here. We decided to meet again in ten days."

"Did you tell him about the mess upon arriving here from parts unknown?" asked Mother Nature.

"No. He hardly asked me anything. That suggests he already knew about the implants, Fantheon, everything. As I think the lawyer Robert Austin does as well."

"But then I told him I was really only nine years old and I had yet to finish elementary school. I also asked if he knew of a place nearby where I could buy some gelato, and if he knew where I could get a dog. I asked if he knew where I could get a book about girls, since most of them didn't seem to make any sense, and if anyone around there knew how to make pasta and risotto? And oh yeah, I asked, 'What is a Ph.D.?'"

"You actually asked him that?" She said.

"I wanted to. Still do. I am going to walk around now and see if I can find a playground." Mother Nature's mouth dropped open in surprise. "Just kidding, my dear," Atlas chuckled.

Chapter Three

Empathy, Truth, Tolerance, Intelligence

**55 years later
The First Gene Edits are Designed For Earth
The Year 1792**

"My goodness, you look tired. Come over here a while and sit." Atlas told Mother Nature as they sat in the living room of the cottage.

She responded, "It's the gene injection project for Earth, of course. I have slaved over this thing for 23 years and we are not even halfway to completion. Admittedly, it has been a part-time endeavor, but still I thought we would be further along by now." She sighed and continued, "At least we have defined what we need for the human aggression problem, which is top priority. You recall how we finally got it right without making the people too passive," said Mother Nature.

"Yes and I recall that was when you built the maze for the rats to figure out. And there were rat wars between the different colored rats. But isn't aggression the gene that everyone wanted to pass on?" Atlas asked.

"Yes it was, but it worked out so quickly and nicely. The key characteristic for rats is quite rare. The DNA for a rat is at least 95% the same as human DNA."

"That is amazing," said Atlas. "How can a rat have the same or nearly the same basic building plan as a human?"

Mother Nature said, "It's because we are both mammals. We both have skeletons and hearts that pump blood. We both have similar digestive systems. We both breathe air and have lungs, we can both see and hear and feel and make decisions with a brain if we are threatened or need food or help."

"I suppose we have lot more work to do with aggression." said Atlas.

Mother Nature sighed and said, "I just finished defining all that is required for dealing with aggression alone. As you recall, we assume that a reduction of aggression will result from strengthening two genes: empathy and tolerance, assuming such genes actually exist. But we are focusing on aggression itself at first. In any case, our final product will be a huge set of instructions. We are years away from completion." She continued, "There is a lot of technical literature on aggression. For example, specific genes have been identified, which have been shown to carry the aggression trait down to individuals. One such gene is called the MAUA gene. This little guy is responsible for the production of the protein monoamine oxide which allows the metabolizing of the neurotransmitters serotonin and dopamine. But if this gene is not working properly we can get increased or excessive levels of serotonin which has a calming influence and low levels have been tied to a reduction of control over impulsive behavior."

"That sounds terribly complicated," said Atlas. "Yes, of course, it is complicated and we have not yet even touched the more subtle human character problems such as honesty or empathy.

"How are we coming with those?" asked Alas. "They are a huge problem. We find that aggression is defined by several genes. But you can't get a measure of human empathy, truth or honesty, or tolerance from a rat or from any other animal. But they might help with intelligence. On the other hand, we have seen papers on several studies by others on personality traits. Already fairly well studied are: extroversion, agreeableness, openness, conscientiousness, and neuroticism."

"But these properties are not going to be included in the research, are they? Something else must be bothering you."

"This is true. We have two big problems. The environment and heritability. A gene could be ignored because of the influence on the outside or from strong environmental factors or it simply is not passed on to children. This last one is called heritability. Our genes and gene combinations get passed on to our children. We have a single opportunity to introduce our gene edits. I'm talking about a large gene edit on a great many young people sometime before they marry. The implant could be successful by implanting any the of the four issues involved into male and female chromosomes."

"Okay, define 'chromosome' for me," said Atlas.

"Chromosomes are thread-like structures located inside the nucleus of animal and plant cells. Each chromosome is made of protein and a single DNA molecule. Passed from parents to offspring, as you know, DNA contains the specific instructions that make each type of living creature unique."

"More," said Atlas"

"When a husband and wife have children, the husband passes down the well known Y-chromosome and an X-chromosome. These are the sex chromosomes. The couple also each pass down genes for traits like eye and hair color. The female has two X type chromosomes. The male has one X and one Y. But the Y from the male may have only 75 genes while the Xs have 700 or more genes."

Atlas said, "Let me summarize...The female has two different Xs. The male has an X and Y. They require a pair."

"Yes," said Mother Nature, nodding her head. "A male child results from pairing the Y-chromosome with a female X type. A female arises from pairing the male X to a female X so that a female has both types of X-chromosome. From this it would appear that the Y-chromosome need not be implanted."

"So a new baby boy has his eye and hair color and other physical attributes selected by the mother," said Atlas. He continued, "One thing is clear from all this. You and I need to hit the road with some first class presentations and solid funding so we can turn on the Universities toward many of these questions and gain a better understanding of how to proceed with gene editing and gene improvements."

"I could not agree more," said Mother Nature and she jumped out of her chair and into her friend's lap, playing kissy face until Atlas felt something growing and immediately swooped up his sweet Missy and carried her to his bedroom. Atlas was aware of a very discrete and frightening problem that Mother Nature had recently discovered in her DNA analysis. He agreed with her position on this problem and made sure she knew he had gotten a vasectomy.

In various speeches given mostly by Mother Nature she would state that once they had established their target gene edits she and her colleagues believed that all humankind should eventually receive the changes, including and without exception, edits for the traits of empathy, truth, tolerance, and higher intelligence. "We will have created a better world where there are no wars, weapons, murders, armies, navies, generals, captains, or military officers," was the phrase she used to conclude her quite convincing speeches.

The new gene traits would be enforced, but not by some agency ordering people around, but because one's body and the mind inside wanted to obey their own set of values and ethics. If a person lied, the next time he found himself in a crowd of people he would urinate all over himself. Or say, a person had negotiated a crooked business contract to swindle someone out of money, upon signing the agreement that person's face would immediately turn red and saliva would drip heavily from their mouth and they'd vomit in front of the person with whom they had been negotiating.

Working tirelessly for the next 15 years, Atlas and Mother Nature—with the help of hundreds of others—finally finished the job. All that was then required to establish a new way of life was an injection of five milliliters of fluid from the syringe of a hypodermic needle into large number of young people.

The date was 1807.

Chapter Four

Terrible Flashes of Light

By the beginning of the 19th Century, Capital City was the most prosperous city on planet Theon. The city was large and affluent with an economy that was largely focused on academic endeavors such as basic research, medical research, finance, new weaponry research and development, as well as research in pharmaceuticals, semiconductors, digital electronics, and space exploration—all supported by five large universities. Indeed, it was a city where people were trying to make life better for themselves, but also a place where many worked hard at making others happy and successful as well.

Like that of Washington D.C. on Earth, Theon's Capital City proudly displayed its wide boulevards, stately government buildings, and famous transportation system which was the finest in their world. The system was so effective that auto traffic became light enough that the people never experienced air pollution. The population spread south to affluent smaller cities. Down farther the people saw a lush green forest on the west and then a vast cool ocean. It was a region with warm winters and cool summers, both ocean moderated.

It is 73 years later and the year is 1810.

Mother Nature and her colleagues knew very early that morning that it was going be to a tough day. They would be working in a huge government facility called Theon Air beginning at 4:00 A.M. The whole day promised a whirlwind of final decisions and last-minute checking before the launch of the spacecraft to Earth. She mulled over the word 'launch'. There would be no actual launch. The Flyer would simply lift off silently into the air like a balloon. It would carry a single passenger—the android Mr. Franklin Steel. All 360 pounds of him.

She would be packing the vials of genes and DNA material and the hypos. Everything was carefully placed in a small refrigerator which was atomic-energy powered, like almost everything on planet Fantheon. Again, Fantheon was a place and society said to be at least a million years ahead of Theon in science and technology.

At 15 light-years distant, planet Fantheon was not exactly close by. All other planets were even further away. There was no way people on Theon or Fantheon could travel that far in one lifetime. In other words, they couldn't be visited by actual living beings from another planet. But they could communicate. Fantheon had developed a remarkable communication technology between themselves and Theon. Both governments could routinely make phone calls with a mere five minute delay. All information was automatically translated in both directions. Theon would frequently be building some marvelous machine, according to Fantheon's detailed specifications, even though those on Theon might not have the foggiest idea of how it worked.

Steel and his spacecraft had been designed at Fantheon. But why do this for Theon? It was suspected that Theon satisfied the need of those on Fantheon who yearned to take care of children.

Now Mother Nature was remembering her concern about the ethics of this mission: traveling to another planet—that is, planet Earth—and leave with them a steel android, who would proceed to implant genes and DNA into some 400 or 500 young people. The implant was designed to eventually cause complete replacement of the current species of human—Homo sapiens. The new people would be less aggressive and more intelligent. Less likely to go to war. Less likely to plunder their own planet. But all this without their permission or knowledge. This last element was very bothersome to Mother Nature.

Mother Nature had driven the twelve miles to the plant and was parked and inside by 3:45 A.M.

Knowing that he was in the plant that day as well, she eventually found and confronted Senator Barrett, who was a strong advocate of what she was about to do. She found him in his office and registered her doubts about proceeding without Earth's permission.

He looked her straight in her eyes and said, "Come with me. Let's hit this issue head on."

The Senator, a large man about fifty years old, in a tailored black suit and red tie, rose from his chair, walked to the door and motioned for her to follow. Some 20 feet down a wide hall, he found his driver. Moments later the threesome stepped out of the building and walked over to a large black limousine parked by the curb. Senator Barrett and the lady got into the back seat.

Mother Nature looked over to the Senator and said, "Sir, this reminds me that we here on Theon are perhaps 200 years ahead of Earth in the development of technology, industry, medicine, and science. They, at present, have no automobiles or aircraft."

"Yes, that's true, but by the middle of the 20th century they will have them, as well as atomic bombs and air pollution and I am not convinced that they can handle it," said the Senator with intensity.

The Senator told the driver to take them to the Museum of Technology. He had phoned ahead and arranged to have his guest and himself visit the deep space exhibit. The two arrived at the building, exited the car and walked into the building and up to a front reception desk. The driver drove to a spacious garage and parked.

At the reception desk, the Senator announced that he wanted to see the new deep space exhibit. He said that he would need some help with the equipment and asked if they would tell Major Denison he had arrived.

The person at the desk answered "Yes, Sir" and off they went down a long hall and into a somewhat darkened auditorium. Denison appeared and immediately told everyone, "Welcome. Please be seated." He explained that a technician would be there shortly.

Looking around the place, to Mother Nature it seemed to be essentially a planetarium where light shows about the fundamentals of astronomy take place.

The technician arrived. The Senator took the technician aside for a few minutes, so no one could hear their discussion. Mother Nature listened but heard only a "Yes, sir". Then he and the Senator walked back to where she was sitting. The young technician began describing and explaining the system. He stated that he could set everything up with the remote control in his hand.

He looked down at his small audience and said "Hello, Miss. My name is Gordon Soren. Before we proceed I need to inform you that I must record this session and make a record of any visitors." While holding his remote control toward Mother Nature he announced, "Please state your name."

She looked at him and calmly said, "Mother Nature."

"No, I mean your real name," replied the technician.

The Senator stood up and barked, "That is her real name! Now let's get on with this."

"Your name is Mother Nature?"

"Yes."

"All right, do you solemnly swear that you will not reveal the information you are about to see regarding flashes of light throughout the universe and their likely origin?"

"Of course not! I am not going to reveal something I have never seen or heard about. Senator, what in the hell is going on here?"

"Mr. Soren, I am ordering you to proceed. I will take full responsibility for my colleague." said the senator angrily.

"Yes, Senator." The technician cleared his throat and said, "We have a wide-angle telescope in a stationary orbit around Theon. It is designed, using filters, to sense the light given off by very high-temperature heavy atoms such as those from plutonium and uranium. I will now activate the wide-angle telescope and darken the room. You've probably noticed the machine in the center of the room. It will project the light detected by the telescope onto the ceiling. Again, it will only show the light given off by certain heavy atomic explosions. The light from stars and suns originates from fusion of hydrogen and helium and emits light at very different wave lengths which do not flash on and off. You will note that we see only brief flashes. The rate is around one per minute. In one year, that would be about one half million. Given the specific spectra there is little doubt about their origin. These lights are from planets destroying themselves in an all-out atomic war. We may also conclude that in some species akin to Homo sapiens, found on planet Earth, this is a common occurrence in the development in the evolution of humans."

After the meeting, the Senator and his guest returned to the car and they headed back to the plant. Back at the plant the Senator, with a captive audience, began his scheduled lecture. "We have seen what is likely to happen to planet Earth unless we intervene. Within only a few centuries they will have stripped the planet of natural resources, polluted the oceans, destroyed the forests, and created a society with living conditions ranging from living in mansions with servants, to those homeless and sleeping on city sidewalks and stealing food."

He continued, "That will never happen here. We already have a world government. We have no wars. If I have my way, we soon will have no one without a quality place to live."

It was about 7:30 P.M. when Mother Nature was finally dropped off in front of her house, exhausted and upset. She stepped out of the limousine and slowly walked up her front sidewalk. She was met by Atlas as she approached the front door. He handed her a glass of wine. He gently picked her up and carried her through the house, out the back doors and ever so carefully placed her in a lawn chair on the grass. He sat down next to her.

She said, "I am almost too tired to talk. " But she had to tell Atlas about the flashes of light. "Atlas, I've just seen saw the most dreadful thing I have ever seen in my life."

Atlas replied, "I think I know. And I am not surprised. You saw Barrett's exploding planet demonstration! I heard about that."

"Senator Barrett took me to our Museum of Technology. They have this wide-angle telescope in orbit. It is designed to pick up the light generated from planets that are blowing themselves up with atomic bombs in a god-awful war. They get over half a million flashes of light a year. He blames–"

Atlas interrupted, "Wait, don't tell me. He believes in the widely discussed sordid and disastrous evolution of Homo sapiens."

"That is correct," she replied.

"Wait! You said atomic bombs? If these people are determined to destroy everything, they would use hydrogen bombs, not atomic bombs. They release one thousand times more energy per second. But of course, if that were true how would you find these little blips when the stars and suns operate by the same process of fusion and emit a thousand times more energy than a bomb? There is no way to sort them out from the star light. I bet they wanted you to sign some papers saying you would keep this information secret. You have heard the word 'hoax'?"

"Oh, my goodness, Atlas, this could be part of the Senator's game to show our superiority with our world government and so forth," said Mother Nature.

"It's probably more serious than that." he mused, and then added, "By the way, tell me more about Mr. Steel. The android that you mentioned yesterday." said Atlas.

Mother Nature explained, "He is meant to look and sound like a large and very strong male, but he's made of steel, motors, bearings, wire, cables, semiconductors, magnets, electronics, and so forth. He has no blood, no cells, nothing resembling anything living. His energy comes from a plutonium fission reactor. He needs no other fuel. He produces no liquid or solid waste. The energy source will run for 500 years without the need for more plutonium. He is programmed to perform one task. He can be creative or clever if necessary to do his job. He can even change his personality if it will help. He cannot attack a human unless threatened."

"That is certainly a needed feature," said Atlas.

Mother Nature continued, "He can turn himself off and on over any period and not care. Can you imagine turning yourself off for a hundred years and then someone pushes restart?"

"No, but that is what will have to happen on the trip to Earth," said Atlas.

"But if he were human and his start button were pushed after a hundred years, nothing would happen. That's for sure. Even if it were you or me?" she stated.

"For us, who knows? Let's not find out."

"Good idea." She paused a moment and then continued. "The only way you can get him to do something else is through a code number. You simply say it and then tell him about his next assignment. He cannot complain. He has no interest in sex, praise or feeling good." She added, "Oh yes, what's more is that the Fantheon engineering group told us that Steel must be referred to using the pronoun 'he' and never 'it'."

"That is probably the most amazing thing I've ever heard. It strengthens my theory," said Atlas.

"What theory?" asked Mother Nature.

"For that, I need just a little more time," said Atlas.

Chapter Five

Landing on Planet Earth

The Year 1910

The size of a school bus, the spacecraft had been traveling about one hundred years through the vacuum of space at almost 50,000 miles per second, a speed which would have killed a human passenger in just a few seconds, but did not bother the two hearing, speaking and thinking beings inside. One was Steel, the almost-sentient android. The other was a speaking and thinking being in charge of navigation and maintenance of the craft. This being was contained in two racks of electronics, one near the cockpit on the right-hand side of the vessel and another rack under the floor. This being was Mr. Rocket.

"Mr. Steel! Mr. Steel! Time to wake up. Time to wake up. We are only 30 minutes from planet Earth," said the deep voice of Mr. Rocket.

Steel replied, "Yes, thank you. I can see that. How are we for fuel?"

"Looking good. We reached our target speed of 46,500 miles per second after two years and then moved through the vacuum of space at speed. No problem. We still have about 590 kg of plutonium. I dropped the temperature to 5°C. That work for you Steel?" said Rocket.

"Call me Captain. I am in charge here."

"Okay," replied Rocket's voice.

"Good." said Steel.

"Right, Captain," said Rocket.

Steel said, "Now, let's go over what needs to happen here. You should fly around very high so that no one down on the surface will see our ship. Pinpoint our location and then go to the northern continent, that is the narrower one. We want to go to the smaller one which has large oceans on both sides. Find the one that is called United States on our map. Fly around and check out areas in the middle. Find the vast forests. Way up on the northern zone there is much ice and snow. Note that to the right of center is a huge body of water and below that you will see smaller lakes."

"These lakes? They stay the same size all the time?" asked Rocket.

"Yes. On all the maps they are always the same." Steel paused a few seconds and then continued. "Just above the smaller lakes is a place where we can probably make our campsite. You'll need to go down there at low altitude and check that there are no humans around. We must, of course, find an area where no people are living now or would likely be living in the future. This area is probably too cold in the winters for them. Then try to find a tall mountainside of stone. We can excavate into the mountain and make a safe place for the Flyer and for our laboratory. You remember that we have brought a nuclear powered excavator. We—that is, I—will have to dig out space in the mountain for everything. We will have to find a place that is secret. I am thinking this should take maybe three months. Okay? While you do this, I must do some maintenance on my body. It has been 100 years."

"Yes Captain," replied Rocket. "I also have some maintenance duties." A cabinet door opened inside the Flyer and a small robot around two feet tall rolled out. "We have some circuit boards to check and recalibrate."

It did not take Rocket long to find a suitable location for the laboratory. He noticed a forested mountain with one side that was quite steep, facing South and free of trees. With the atomizer ray gun, he cleared a space in front large enough to dock their spacecraft for a while. Rocket then parked the Flyer in the clearing.

Steel exited the Flyer, walked over to the mountainside and prodded it with a stick. He measured the temperature. It was 6.67 °C. He looked over to Rocket and said: "Excellent. This place will work."

Rocket scanned the 12 video sensors placed around the ship. He considered launching the armed drone, but decided it was too early.

Steel returned to his lecture mode. "Next, we must find a source of supplies—copper wire, solvents, hardware and the like. Here is what I propose we do: put the flyer in stealth mode—that is, use only the silent antigravity engines to locate some nearby towns. After dark, at around 2:00 A.M., creep down their streets looking for likely stores and businesses. Look for newspapers sold in racks along the streets. Pick up a few with your extension arm. I will go through them and try to find stores that might have what we need. I will make a list of places to check out. You can drop me off at likely places. I will break in and simply take what we need. You can drop down in the street in front and pick me up. I will leave some gold coins in compensation for what I've taken."

Several days later, Rocket and Steel were slowly moving down a street in Bangor, Maine—a booming town on the Atlantic Coast. In front of one store, they noticed a sign which listed dozens of items, including copper wire and wood alcohol. Steel thought maybe they were in luck with the wire. On another street Steel had spotted a Telegraph and Telephone Office.

"Okay. Stop in front of that hardware store." Steel jumped out of the Flyer carrying a large canvas bag. He opened the locked front door of the store in his usual fashion. He simply grabbed the doorknob and ripped out the entire mechanism. In less than five minutes he was on his way back out, the bag completely full. He was a few feet from the side entrance to the Flyer when a man burst out through the mangled front door, yelling and shaking his fist.

"Hey you! Wait jest a minute, Feller. Yeah, you with the bag. What's yawl got in there? Stuff from ma store?"

"Sir! I've left coins on the counter," yelled Steel.

"Stuff you ain't paid for? I tell you one damn thang. I didn't come up from South Carolina to get robbed. No Sur. No Sirreee."

"Mr. store owner. You are not listening! I paid for the items in the bag!" screamed Steel, as loud as he could.

"See this here long metal gun? This here Springfield? Best rifle in the world! Loaded with .50 caliber cartridges. Really biggons. Ahl bet it'll put a hole clean through one side and out the other of that contraption you're in."

Rocket spoke in an alarmed tone to the captain. "Captain, if this man fires his weapon and a bullet penetrates the computer, this mission is over. The Flyer is not designed for combat. We can't even pressurize the interior for humans. I think I'd better take care of this man."

Steel remained silent. Thinking.

A narrow metal barrel appeared from the side of the Flyer. It lined up, pointing straight at the man with the rifle. A hot liquid was dispensed onto the poor store owner.

Within milliseconds what had been a man became a white-hot sphere which leapt away from the street, expanding as it raced upward. By the time it was five hundred feet in diameter it was composed of simple gas molecules such as nitrogen, oxygen and carbon dioxide. Other elements became simple oxides such as the ordinary oxides of iron, calcium or magnesium. Sulfur and phosphorus could easily make negatively charged sulphates and so could phosphates, bouncing around until they bumped into eager partners such as positively charged magnesium, calcium or even small amounts of iron. These everyday compounds assimilated into everyday stuff. There was no DNA, no sugars, no proteins. There was absolutely nothing unique that might be construed as originating from a human person. The hot cloud drifted in the wind, cooled and scattered its ordinary dust with the similar constituents of ordinary dirt.

A boy about nine years old ran out the front door of the store shouting, "Dad! Dad! Da—". Another hot sphere appeared over the sidewalk where the boy once stood.

The Flyer from another world then silently and slowly drifted down the street. "I did not know we had such a weapon," said Steel.

Rocket replied in his usual casual tone, "Really? I've known about it, but I never thought we would have to use it."

"Next time, if there ever is one, let me make the decision to fire. Okay?"

"Sure, no problem," said Rocket, while thinking to himself, *When would that be—after we are both dead?*

Chapter Six

The First Gene Implant

Mr. Steel Goes to Town

"Mr. Rocket, it seems to me that we have made excellent progress during our first three months here on Planet Earth. We have excavated a large space in the mountainside, which should be enough for lab needs and your parking space. We have constructed and placed a very heavy log door in front. It can be opened only by sliding it to one side along a rough slot at the bottom. I don't think even several humans could move it. I estimate it weighs 3,000 pounds. A person would have to push it to one side at least three feet before a human could get by. What do you think?"

"No, I don't believe even several humans could move the door. Even if they managed to get in, they would not find much—lab glassware, some ordinary chemicals. I have the gene vials here with me in the refrigerator in the Flyer."

"Good. Tomorrow let's go to Bangor and see if we can find some school children to start our gene dose program. It is still quite cold here so I need to buy a large and heavy coat so I don't stand out while walking around outside."

"Yes, you must not stand out! By the way, you are getting very good at applying your makeup. You look almost like a human. But I may not be the best judge for such a thing." said Rocket.

March 15, 1910

They noticed a large clear area in the forest near Bangor and set the Flyer down. Steel then exited the Flyer and walked to town, which took about 30 minutes. He carried a suitcase, with two changes of clothes and, of course, the vials of gene material. A large bag on his back contained an expensive hobby telescope.

In order to give the appearance of normalcy, Steel had rented a room at the Charles Inn. Steel was strolling casually down Ocean Ave. sporting his new dark grey 100% wool overcoat. He had just purchased it in a men's clothing store. He had told the clerk, after handing him a new-looking gold coin marked $20, that he would soon be moving to Bangor and that he had two teenage girls who were ready for high school. Steel asked if there was a high school close to the downtown area, since he was planning to buy or build in this area. The clerk said he was in luck. Right in front, on Ocean Avenue, there was a new subdivision under construction. Steel thanked him and told him that he was glad the clerk wasn't too bothered by his appearance—his face—that he was healing from a serious burn. The clerk replied that he had hardly even noticed. Steel thanked him again and began his walk down Ocean Avenue.

There was a concrete sidewalk on either side of a wide street which was still frozen. Steel thought that the ice was fortuitous as it would prevent the muddy mess of an unpaved surface. He noticed an impressive red brick building. In front of the building a masonry sign read 'Bangor High School'. Steel walked inside.

Eventually he found a glass fronted cabinet with a list of teachers' names, along with their subjects and room numbers. He noted that a Mr. Ronald Simpson taught Science in Room 209. Assuming this must be on the second floor he headed up the stairs at the end of the hall. Glancing through glass in the upper part of a door he saw a room full of students sitting in their wooden desks attached to chairs. Down the hall he saw a table stacked high with more desks. The time—which he always knew down to the second—showed that it was likely the class would be over in eleven minutes. He saw a wooden bench down the hall and walked over to it, jumped up a little and essentially threw himself onto the bench. The bench, not designed for a 360 pound android plus his falling inertia, exploded with a loud bang like a gun shot. Steel, with remarkable speed, leapt up and began racing down the hall toward the table stacked high with student desks and raked them off the table with a swoop of his arm. Some were still airborne as Steel ran down the stairs. He heard them crashing to the floor. One was careening down the stairs right behind him. Finally, he was all the way down, standing in the first floor hall looking up as if wondering, *What in the hell is going on up there?*

When Science teacher Simpson heard the big noise, he listened a few seconds longer and told his class "Be calm, just stay put a minute." He told the class that he would take a look out in the hall and see what had happened. He left the classroom, walked out into the hall and looked nervously both ways. It looked much safer to the left, away from the end where desk chairs were strewn everywhere. Reentering the classroom, he announced, "Okay. Class is dismissed. I want everyone to go left and use the east end stairs to calmly exit the building." The bewildered students all stood up and scampered out the doors, turned left and raced pell-mell down the hall to the stairs and then outside.

Steel decided it was time to start slowly walking back up the stairs. He was about halfway up when a man peered down at him and said, "Hey there. You see anyone just run down these stairs?"

"Yes, I did!" answered Steel. "I was just coming up when a man with lots of paint splatter on his clothes appeared, racing in panic down the stairs. When I first came in the building I heard a lot of noise. What was that? Sounded like it was coming from the second floor?"

The Science teacher answered, "Yes, it was a terrible noise. Somebody has scattered a large stack of desk chairs all over the place. Had to dismiss my class. By the way, my name is Ronald Simpson. I teach Science here," and he extended his hand.

"Nice to know you," answered Steel as he lowered his head. He then looked back at Simpson and continued, "I am always embarrassed at moments like this. But I've been told by my doctors to not shake hands. I was recently badly burned. You can probably see the makeup on my face. My hands are even worse. My name is Franklin Steel."

Simpson graciously answered, "Sorry to hear that. No need to shake hands." Steel seized his opportunity and said, "It's clear that you're quite busy but I came here to the high school today especially to meet you, Mr. Simpson."

"Simpson paused and looked again at the big man. "Alright, I'll give you a moment in the teachers' lounge where we can talk. But first I must call the police. You'll have to wait." He indicated a bench nearby and took off.

It was almost an hour before Simpson returned. He showed Steel to the teachers' lounge, sat down on a battered sofa, ran a hand through his hair and said, "Okay that's done. Everything's under control. What can I do for you, Mr. Steel?"

Steel began, "I arrived here from London about a week ago. Before my family arrives I'd like to have everything ready for them. I have a wife and two teenage sons." He then paused for a moment, remembering that he had said daughters to the shopkeeper. *Best keep my story consistent*, he thought.

"Go on," said Simpson.

Steel continued, "They are both quite interested in Science. Perhaps your class is too advanced for them, or maybe not advanced enough. I was wondering if I could sit in on a few classes. I'd sit at the back and never say a word. You could tell the class that I am a writer, which is what I more or less am. More specifically, I work for a large publishing firm where I do fact-checking and research into what is new in the world, especially in science. Which brings me to another reason I wanted to speak to you."

Simpson, although quite tired, listened to the man with interest. Steel continued, "I am not sure how to broach the next topic, but perhaps I should ask first—do you cover Astronomy in your class?"

"Yes, to some extent," said Simpson. He then elaborated, "We cover what is known about our solar system and the orbital equations. But if you are talking about Albert Einstein's theory of special relativity published five years ago and the theoretical results and empirical findings obtained by Michelson, Lorentz, Poe and others such as Max Plank, we think most of that is too new and too complicated for our class."

"Yes, of course, I would agree." answered Steel. "Here is what I would like you to consider. I propose that you and maybe two of your best students examine a telescope I've brought from London. My sons found the thing in an abandoned barn about a year ago. They brought it home and we've been marveling over the thing ever since."

Simpson straightened up a bit and said. "Hhmm, interesting."

Steel went on, "Oh yes, it has some brass terminals marked plus and minus 12V. Here the boys got lucky. In a Science class at their school, they had been making the so-called Daniel Cell, which uses copper and zinc electrodes. By refurbishing 11 of those and connecting them in series they created a 12V power supply. As soon as this was attached, the telescope went into its magic mode."

Steel continued as an ever more curious Simpson leaned in closer. "Even more puzzling is this: Below the keyboard is a metal chamber full of hundreds of tiny parts, all wired and soldered together into a very complex circuit. We assume that somehow this system directs and controls the telescope positioning."

"Seems impossible," said Simpson.

"Yes, it does. But even more bizarre is the fact that none of these parts, as far as we can tell, have ever been seen in any device or in any system on this planet. It's a little scary."

"Why scary? asked Simpson.

"I hope that someday, if I use the telescope outside, little green men with ray guns won't walk up and announce, 'THAT IS OUR TELESCOPE!'"

"I am sorry, but there are no green men here in Bangor."

"Are you sure?"

"By last count we have only white, brown and black men," Simpson said, laughing. "Hey, if you are available perhaps you can bring the telescope to my house tomorrow night. Say 8:00 P.M.? I'd love to take a look at it."

"Okay. Great. I will be there." Steel answered.

"I think I have enough batteries in my workshop to provide 12 volts. I'm sure my son Albert would love to see it. He could invite his friend Henry as well. They are both quite interested in Astronomy. Here is a card with my address. It's only five blocks from here."

"Great!" answered Steel. "See you at eight tomorrow might."

Around 7:00 P.M. the next night

Steel was changing his clothes and was essentially nude—if such a term could be used in his case—when a total stranger burst into his room.

"Sorry, I thought...What the hell? Jesus Chr..." the man stammered.

Steel jumped over his bed and had the man's head in his hands in seconds. He whacked the intruder's head up against his chin, instantly knocking him out. He then quickly shut the door and stuffed the unconscious man under his bed. Steel muttered to himself, "This means I will have to speed things up tonight."

8:00 P.M.

Ronald Simpson stood on his front porch and said, "Mr. Steel, right on time! That must be the telescope on your back. Let's go out to the backyard where we can set it up."

"We are in luck, Mr. Simpson. Looks like good weather. No clouds and no cold wind tonight."

Steel laid the bag down and they went through introductions all around. The boys, Albert and Henry, began taking directions from Steel on how to set up the telescope. First they dealt with a heavy tripod which they extended to 3.5 feet, then the telescope itself was attached at its center. He pointed out the six inch mirror inside at the bottom and the eye piece up at other end toward the sky. They then headed back into the workshop to get a small table and the batteries.

Simpson emerged from the back door with a bottle of wine and four glasses. He filled each glass half full, set the glasses down on a table and announced, "I'll be right back."

In a motion so fast that it was a blur, Steel removed a small bottle from his jacket pocket, opened it, and extracted a small amount of the dark liquid with an eye dropper. He then dropped one ml into each wine glass. In a flash he put everything back into his pocket.

Simpson bolted through the back door and announced, "Okay everyone, it's time for a toast." The boys quickly appeared from the workshop. Simpson handed everyone a glass and loudly said, "Here is a toast to our new friend, Mr. Steel, my son Albert, and his friend Henry. May they all make amazing discoveries with this new telescope." Everyone then took a long sip of wine.

After some five minutes and complaining of a sudden tiredness, three members of the group were fast asleep in lawn chairs. Steel then injected into each young man a measured amount of the gene altering liquid, using a very small needle which left an undetectable entry point.

Steel then left the Simpson property, leaving the telescope there. He collected his luggage which he had stashed in a wooded spot off the road and returned to the Flyer.

Five days later back in their hideout, Steel and Rocket received the following series of messages from Mother Nature on Planet Theon:

'Mr. Steel, we are all very impressed with your progress upon reaching Planet Earth. But it is clear now that putting gene implants into desirable candidates is more complex than we were thinking. You were right in making a quick exit from Bangor. Your early detection and identification would have been a disaster.

On the other hand, we have changed our plans as to how you should proceed during the next several years. Some of us are concerned that we have not properly established that the gene material is completely safe for humans on Earth. Please operate for some years as follows: Implant 100 people (mainly infants) and track their progress for the next 30 to 40 years. We must establish empirically that this program is clearly beneficial and causes no unwanted anomalies. Then we can proceed with the final 400 subjects.

As we discussed before, continue to select people that appear healthy—people who live in reasonably well-maintained homes and towns and are employed. This should help. And ask people around town how the local hospital is doing. You could say you get the flu from time to time.

Finally, it would be wise to establish other home bases for the Flyer. But no hurry.

Best wishes and regards,
Mother Nature

Chapter Seven

Fifty years of Gene Implants

The Year 1961

From the messages of Mother Nature:

Steel, you have done extremely well.

Over 200 people have received our gene modifier and the results remain outstanding—an excellent job over the past 50 years. Seven gene modification recipients have received the Nobel Prize. Fifty have been very successful—if not famous—in their fields. None have shown extreme behaviors. There are no criminals or any with mental disorders. Six perished in World War Two.

We now seek data on the effects of the gene cocktail on slightly older people, those in their early twenties. We expect fewer benefits here but it's important to find out more quantitatively. We will thus be sending exact names and locations for the next recipients.

Penn State University
Pennsylvania 1960

About 150 miles northwest of Philadelphia lies the massive Penn State University. Across the main drag Beaver Avenue, we find Sauers Harvest Café.

Good friends Katy Rogers and Robert Mann, both third year students, had been going there most Friday afternoons for a late lunch together. This had been going on for about two months. The attraction was mainly from Robert's side. He had found that math major Katy could help him understand math complexities that came up in flight simulation equations he was studying in his major in Aeronautics.

A large man in black trousers and a white shirt approached with a tray holding two glasses of wine. He stopped at their table said, "The owner has noticed your regular appearance and would like to show his appreciation by offering some wine at no charge. How does that sound?"

Robert said, "Great! Thank you."

The man placed a wine glass in front of the lady and one in front of Robert and quickly turned and walked away.

They each took a sip.

In precisely two minutes the big man was back. The few other patrons in the room were not paying attention. He came up behind the lady and moved his mouth as if he were saying something but made no sound. Using the tray as a visual shield he pulled her shirt collar back and quickly inserted the needle into her neck.

With a friendly face and some fake soundless speaking, he moved behind the man and performed the same process. Whirling around, Steel walked out of the café.

Ten minutes later the regular waiter was gently slapping Robert's face. "Sir! Sir! Your lunch is here."

He looked over at Katy who was struggling to keep her eyes open and said, "Let's go. I am a zombie." Robert dropped $10 on the table.

They staggered out, crossed the main road and fell together under a big tree, both asleep before they hit the ground.

Almost two years later

Robert was 22 years old and close to completing his BS in Aeronautics at Penn State. The massive space program called NASA had started four years before that, and Penn State with their aero-engineering program was already receiving funding for reliability evaluations of the many and various state-of-the-art components used in building spacecrafts. Robert was working in a lab for one of his professors. He had already been accepted by MIT for graduate work but wanted to first earn some money to help with expenses. His parents were paying for most of his college expenses.

The year was 1962. That was the year President John Kennedy and his brother Robert out-foxed Soviet premier Nikita Khrushchev, thus avoiding the possibility of a nuclear war and world catastrophe. The event was called the Cuban Missile Crisis.

The young Robert Mann had noticed that one Miss Katy Rogers was now busying herself in the lab. She was working for the same Professor that he reported to. Katy had just received her degree in Math.

As the two young people moved about the lab that day, he could not keep his eyes off her. During the past several months somehow she had changed. *Just look at her*, he thought—perfect white teeth, long black glossy hair, and a fluidity of motion that only a female could exhibit.

It was about 8:00 P.M. and both Robert and Katy were busy with their projects. The professor had asked them both to complete their projects ASAP. They happened to come together at the computer terminal table. Across from the terminals was a huge IBM Main-Frame behind glass walls. They were 14 years away from the introduction of the first desktop personal computer.

Looking at his friend Katy, Robert asked "What do you think of the monster computer?"

"I'm not sure. We had an introductory class about it a few months ago. It's a nightmare to program. You have to make all these paper cards full of little holes called punch cards. Maybe when they get that fixed, I will give it another try. In the meantime I have question for you. How is your sex life?"

Robert stood a little straighter and said, "Sex life? What do you mean sex life? I have no sex life!"

"No sex life? I am not surprised. Follow me." Katy took his hand and off they went toward a storeroom door a short distance down the main hall. Both inside, Katy pressed a nearby chair up under the door handle. "Don't you just hate interruptions when you're having fun?" she asked.

"Well, I suppose they could be annoying or maybe embarrassing?" said Robert.

Katy replied, "Yes, indeed. Embarrassing, very embarrassing. Okay, my good friend with no sex life." She pointed, "Please scoot over there and sit down on the on edge of that desk."

Backing up, he reached the desk. Placing his palms down on its surface, he scooted up and onto the desktop.

"No sex life, huh?" Pleased with her progress so far, a grinning Katy Rogers moved up to her boyfriend and in an instant had loosed his belt, undone the top button on his jeans, reached down low and said "Okay, scoot up a little." She pulled his jeans down and off and flung them on to the left side of the desk. She then, as quick as an electric spark, produced a similar near instantaneous removal of his underwear. "Now that's better. Your man down there can breathe now. And my goodness, he's pretty big. Must have been pretty tight down there. Maybe he needs a massage."

Roger was moaning, "Oh my God. Oh my God. Oh my God. Oh my God." Looking down all he could see was the back of her head and her lustrous dark hair.

From dozens of girl-talks over several years Katy knew in detail how men reacted to sex in similar ways and at critical times. During real sex, men invariably exhibit similar signals after which they proceed to the finish with nearly exactly the same timing. Katy knew in advance how this would proceed.

Roger suddenly stiffened. "Oh my God. Oh my God."

She quickly rose up and pulled back some. She grabbed his junk with both hands and performed a few pumping actions where upon Roger yelled, "OHH... SHEEEEEIT!" which immediately brought forth a gob of white liquid which shot out like it had just erupted from a water cannon on a fire boat. It flew over the aisle and landed with a wet sounding plop on the soapstone countertop across from their area.

Grinning, Katy said, "Well. That was really something." She reached behind her, grabbed a towel and handed it to Roger who was breathing loudly as if he had just arrived at the finish line after a five-mile marathon. He staggered over to a nearby chair and sat down hard as if falling from a great height.

"Okay. So now." She tried to hold back a giggle. "You now have a sex life. How was it"?

Roger was still winding down, his head back, eyes shut. He croaked, "It was different."

They sat quietly. Not speaking. The silence grew. It filled the room…and filled the room and filled the room. Katy bought her hands slowly to her eyes, which were streaming with tears. Sobbing, she whispered, "What have I done?" A black transient of fear rippled through her body. "What I have I done?"

She could hear her friend Alice, in her head, lecturing and wagging her finger, warning her. 'Are you kidding me? You are going to sit this guy down on a desk, a person you barely even know, a guy whom you have never even seen in a bathing suit. And not just any guy—this is the dreamboat you want to marry. You are going to sit him down on a desk, whisk off his clothes until he's naked like some sort of sex-crazed mental patient and give him a blow job—an event he has no idea is about to happen. And this guy is your dreamboat, the one you want to marry? You can be sure that last part will never happen. He is going to bolt like a frightened wild-turkey whose tail feathers are on fire. You will never see him again.'

Crying, moaning like a wounded animal, Katy whirled around, grabbed her keys off her desktop and ran out of the building toward the parking lot.

She was only feet from her car when a voice from behind said, "Katy. Katy, stop. It's okay. Just stop."

She felt a hand on her shoulder and stopped and turned. It was Robert. She realized he must have jumped up and began chasing her the second she burst through the building doors. She looked at him and sobbed. "What have I done? You must think I'm–"

"Katy, don't worry. There's no problem. You've got balls. I mean you have nerve, spunk, spirit, assurance… strength, you know…audacity. And that is what I like about you. Anyway. If I hadn't wanted to play your game, I would have stopped you."

Katy turned and opened her car door, grabbed a little towel she kept in her door pocket, and returned wiping her still wet and smudged face.

Robert continued, "Katy, how about we walk over to that bench and sit down?" He pointed to a cast iron metal park bench. She nodded. He took her hand and off they went. They sat down.

Turning toward Robert, Katy said, "You don't think I have ruined everything? Been crude. Been really gross?"

Robert laughs. "You? Gross? What about me? I'm the one who shot semen in the air in front of his girlfriend." He laughed again. "That probably should go into the all-time super gross column. But the reality of all this is I knew in advance what you were up to. Your friend Alice at Penn State University was worried about you. Called yesterday and told me all about your sex-life scheme. Told me how you had quizzed all these girls and figured out exactly how it would go. She said you were worried that I might to go off to Boston and start my work at MIT and you would never see me again. It was quite a story. I could have, of course, decided in advance that I was not going to do it. But the thing that really intrigued me was why. What was the driving force here? Why such an elaborate scheme? And why me?

"Because you are what I want. What I have to have. You are the only one."

Robert looked at her. "Katy, will you marry me?"

"Of course. How about first thing in the morning?"

Chapter Eight

Implanted Babies
Linda and Jack

Fort Worth, Texas
The Year 2002

Steel had received instructions to implant two infants near a certain high school in Fort Worth, Texas. He had received two specific addresses from Mother Nature. One was on a street called West 7th, another on Bunting Street. Both were about six to eight blocks from a large high school called Arrington Heights.

Steel had learned that the only way to safely perform this operation was to study the neighborhood in detail for several weeks, as well as the habits of the kids' parents. Luckily, he had brought with him from Theon (via Fantheon) a video transmitting system. It was in the Flyer when he left Theon almost 200 years ago. For both addresses he placed an imaging device up on a wooden utility pole. He did this very late at night and had never had a problem.

Back in the Flyer it would take several weeks of study before he could decide how to how proceed.

Eventually it became clear that both families behaved similarly. Around 6 or 7 P.M. on most days a babysitter arrived or sometimes they picked her up. Both parents would then drive away for three to five hours and then return home together. The obvious time for Steel to enter the house was a few minutes after they were gone—assuming, of course, that it was also dark.

Steel decided to proceed and selected the house on West 7th to enter first. He walked about one hour from the Flyer's hiding place near a heavily forested river area. It was summer and still light, so he walked around the neighborhood until it was dark.

He stepped to the front door and wrenched it open, as usual. Walking into the family room he confronted the babysitter who began screaming like an air raid siren. He quietly approached her and gently said that she was in no danger. "Just be quiet and you will not be hurt," he advised. She calmed down. He took the cell phone out of her hands and pulled the land line cable out of the wall.

Outside, the parents had pulled up in the driveway earlier than expected. Albert Grable noted the front door had been damaged and stood wide open. He reached into the glove box and pulled out a shiny silver pistol. His wife Ginger was too frightened to speak. Grable, with gun held out in front of him, raced to the front door and into the house.

"Who in the hell are you?" he said as he saw Steel in his living room.

Steel said nothing and walked toward Grable and the gun. "You better stop right n–" BANG! Grable fired straight into Steel's chest.

Steel grabbed the gun and with his fingers on the barrel, twisted it 90 degrees upward and handed it back to Grable. Steel then turned and took one step back, grabbed one arm of the babysitter and one arm of Mr. Grable, and marched them both down a hall and into a bathroom. He told them to stay there and they would not be harmed.

Steel returned to the family room and picked up a large china cabinet, which he took back down the hall and placed in front of the bathroom door. Steel returned to the family room, lifted a long couch off the floor, took it down the hall and jammed it between the china cabinet and the opposite wall. He then walked over the couch and down the hall to the baby's bedroom. He entered and turned on an overhead light. The baby was asleep in an antique wooden crib. He gently removed the light blanket, laid the baby face down, pulled down her diaper, placed the gene gun barrel on her little butt and fired. This produced the usual little red spot.

The baby was now screaming. He could hear frantic pounding on the bathroom door and a woman screaming outside. He placed the baby back on her back, and calmly turned and left the house through a back door into the backyard. Running, he was quickly out of the neighborhood and on his way to Bunting Street.

Thinking about what just happened, he said to himself, "Under the circumstances that went pretty well. Did the implant. The police will arrive and not believe a word of his story."

Thirty minutes later Steel burst into the home of the Foster family and had little trouble implanting baby Jack Foster.

Chapter Nine

The Planet Theon

Mother Nature

Once a year on Planet Theon Mother Nature opened her gardens to the public. The party was held in the spring, of course. This year the party was just as lavish and well attended as ever. The gardens were in full bloom and a warm breeze gently blew. She was chatting with Atlas when out of the corner of her eye she noticed someone walking firmly and steadily in an unalterable vector directly towards her, apparently coming to see her.

Aware of this as well, Atlas made a quick exit. Turning her head, Mother Nature saw who it was—without doubt the most boring man in the Universe, the hyper-extroverted numbers freak, Chronos, the God of Time.

"Why, Chronos, it is so nice to see you, it's been years," she said politely.

"Hello there, Mother Nature, my wonderful friend. Yes, it has been a year. On Earth that would be 365 days, or 8,760 hours or 525,600 seconds. Don't you just love those numbers? I mention Earth because I hear you are planning an expedition there. Is that true, my dear?"

Mother Nature replied in a friendly tone, "Yes, that is true. However, the expedition to Earth actually started 200 years ago when we launched the spacecraft. But we did hear only a few days ago that they have arrived safely. You know, of course, that messages can be sent much faster than solid objects."

"Oh, my goodness that is so wonderful. You must have hundreds of lovely numbers regarding this. You know I just adore numbers."

"Yes, I know. And you are right, I do need a great many numbers in my work. For example, have you seen my new telescope? It's amazing. Give me a guess for its magnification? Remember, I am using it mostly for studying Earth, which is 4 light-years away."

"Well," said Chronos, "I recall hearing some years ago that if you want to see the planets you would need a 300-power telescope. But, Mother Nature, just how closely would you like to examine Earth?"

"I would like to be able look at things on Earth as close as I can see things here. Just by looking with my unaided eyes."

"Okay, I think I can make a guess." He popped up from his chair, looked around, and noticed Atlas looking at a collection of orchids. He waved and called loudly, "Oh, Atlas! Atlas dear, could you join us a second?"

Atlas immediately headed over to their table. "My dear friend Atlas, you look absolutely scrumptious tonight. My goodness! I was wondering if you would do a calculation for us? I've heard you are quite good at such things. Could you do just one for me? I don't think it will be too difficult."

Taking out a pink handkerchief, Chronos wiped his brow and said "Okay, I want to calculate how many lines, 1/10 of a millimeter wide, would you see by looking at the earth with a 300-power telescope. I know you couldn't really make out such lines. But if you could, what would be the power of the telescope? The earth's diameter is 8000 miles. And the—"

"The answer is 15 trillion. Anything else? No? Nice seeing you Chronos." Atlas turned, took a few steps and vanished.

"Well, that was quick. There is, of course, no telescope with that high a level of magnification. 15 trillion? I don't think so."

Mother Nature looked at her guest and replied, "Okay, how about a number even higher? How about a magnification of say…10 to the 15? Let's count the zeros—000000000000000. That is what I have. I can read a newspaper lying on a sidewalk in New York City."

Chronos gasped, "Ten to the 15? No way!"

"There is a way. You get it designed and delivered free from people who are one or two million years ahead of us in evolution, the people from the planet Fantheon, 15 light years distant. So, unknown to me it had to be assembled here on Theon. Still, it did take 48 years for delivery, but who is in a hurry? I am patient. It is said I have at least another 1,000 years here on Theon."

"That is so amazing. I must hear that again—000000000000000. That is so lovely. But how did they do it?"

"I really wish I knew. It's about the use of anti-matter tachyons that travel through space at 100,000 times the speed of light. Our people here don't understand the physics. It's embarrassing. But still, the Fantheon people give us details for making various devices and remarkable equipment and we follow their directions and they usually work. That is how I got my wonderful telescope. From detailed instructions. There are parts and systems inside that to this day we don't understand."

She paused a moment, then continued, "That reminds me of the harrowing experience a few months ago when it arrived here at our local airport. The controllers had been tracking a quite large spacecraft for hours. I say spacecraft. As far as they knew it was a jet airplane. It was circling at 10,000 feet. The airport traffic controllers could not get anyone to talk to. They were receiving just a recorded message, in our language, saying that they had a large package they needed to deliver to me. Of course, to the military I am no more than a geneticist with a catchy name who works for seed companies. The circling plane just repeated this order over and over, never saying who they were. The situation being unique they called the military, who responded immediately. Within minutes the military arrived in armored troop carriers with other massive vehicles loaded with high-tech weapons and missiles. I ran out on the runway with a major chasing me carrying a gun and yelling at me to stop immediately. The armed vehicles moved toward us."

"Armed vehicles? My goodness! How many?"

"In minutes they had formed a large circle around us. A military officer with lots of stars and ribbons on his jacket left his vehicle and trotted toward us."

Not able to just listen any longer, Chronos offered, "Are these people crazy? Don't they know who you are? A Goddess who has been here since the first Century."

"Quiet now. Shhhh, Chronos. Some do, most do not, some believe I am a genetics consultant with a silly marketing name, a few big government guns seem to accept the first Century story, yes. But very few. I'll tell you about it another time. Getting back to the airport—I was thinking all hell was about to break loose. Then, at an astonishing speed a large spacecraft seemingly dropped out of the sky and landed within the circle of military vehicles. I walked quickly over to the newly arrived military man and told him I was Mother Nature. I asked him to call General Roper and tell him that my telescope had arrived. I told them that Roper knew all about it. He nodded affirmatively. I gave him the number. He said he knew the General. Then a very large door on the spacecraft swung up and open. A heavy crate was then quickly delivered by a robotic system down onto the concrete surface. I walked up to a metal stairway ramp which had just descended from the spacecraft. An odd sounding voice invited me to come inside the craft and come to the cockpit. It became clear at this point that no living beings were on board. Peering down the body of the ship I could see the cockpit—no one was there—and so I left, holding my breath."

"Then I heard a voice which announced, 'Good day to you, Miss Mother Nature. Greetings from President Allister who personally has sent you this gift. In order to confirm its delivery, please grasp the lighted red handle and pull it down toward you.' So, I walked to the cockpit and did as I was told. I grasped a large red lighted metal rod and rotated it down as far as it would go. Nothing happened. I took a deep breath. The voice said 'Thank you, you may now leave the spacecraft.' I left as quickly as I could. I scrambled down the stairs which were immediately drawn back into the craft. I was not two steps away when the whole machine leapt upward with a whoosh of air but no engine noise. It ascended with astonishing speed. The space craft was out of sight before we could even look upward. The army officers both looked at me with astonishment then whirled around and walked away without a word."

Chronos stood next to her, listening with his hand over his mouth in astonishment. "Do go on," he said. "This is simply fascinating!"

"I called my office at the gardens and they arrived with a huge truck and took my present home. On the way home both officers called me and claimed they had arrived at the airport and had seen nothing unusual. Never reached the General. They asked if I had seen something I told them, 'No, it was a total waste of time. Nothing happened.'And that is how I got my new telescope."

Chronos sighed and said, "You have the most fascinating tales to tell! Thank you so much for the wonderful story. Even though I didn't hear any numbers. I like numbers. I have one question. You said it took 100 years to reach planet earth. How did the passengers survive?" asked Chromos.

"Mr. Chronos, that is a good question. We sent an android we've named Mr. Steel. Just him. No other passengers. He is truly remarkable. Covered in stainless steel plates."

"Wonderful! Tell me more. With numbers, please."

"Okay. He weighs 360 pounds and is six feet three inches tall. He uses 250 neodymium-cobalt-iron motors all linked to 250 +/- speed controllers which are operated by a digital computer with 50 Tb of memory. His electric power comes almost directly from a plutonium nuclear reactor from a technology the Fantheons thus far refuse to reveal. Can't really blame them for that. This is probably the most important technical breakthrough in the last 500 years."

Chronos interrupted briefly, "Wow, now that is a number! I love it. An impressive number indeed. 500 years. 500365 days. 122008760 hours. Please, Dear Friend, you have been so kind today. I have only one final question to ask. It is this—you have received so much from the planet Fantheon. Why are they so generous?"

"Alright, I'll tell you. But it requires some background. Maybe not so many numbers. Are you going to listen? Not interrupt?"

"YES YES YES, three times yes," gushed Chronos.

"There are good reasons to believe that the literally billions of planets in the universe have life forms similar to ours. One reason is that we all come from the stars. Let me explain. Our bodies are formed mainly of six elements: hydrogen, oxygen, carbon, nitrogen, a bit of phosphorus for our DNA and finally calcium for bones. These elements account for more than 99% of the atoms inside us. Then we need about 0.85% more composed of another five elements: potassium, sulfur, sodium, chlorine, and magnesium. So, 12 total elements and we are done. The Periodic Table of Elements lists 102 total. We use about 10% of them to make ourselves. Where did the all these elements come from? From exploding stars. At the end of life for a star, it forms a super nova and emits an intense light. We can see these occasionally in the sky, sometimes for a few days. As the star expands and then contracts, it reaches extremely high temperatures where all of the elements are synthesized. The elements then drift out into space. By means of the force of gravity the elements will agglomerate into particles ranging in size from tiny specs to newly forming planets."

"New planets maybe quite hot, even liquid. The denser elements then drift toward the center via forces of gravity or from magnetic forces. Very dense elements such as plutonium and uranium drift more rapidly and can then generate more heat via nuclear reactions. New planets can exhibit intense volcanism for billions of years. Eventually if the planet is not made of gas like Jupiter or so small that its gravity is weak, we could have one just the right size to sustain permanent oceans of water. And after perhaps a billion years when the new planet has cooled down and the volcanoes are no longer constantly blowing their stacks, we might have an infinity of tide pools and various puddles, and ponds of water rich with dissolved carbonates, nitrates, sulfates, phosphates, amides, amino acids, a few proteins, even micro cage-like organic molecules, compound fragments and so on. Each one a little random mini lab that might stumble into creating a compound that could copy itself into more just like it. Once this happened, our survival of the fittest rule took control and our new planet then became busy covering itself with life."

"So, Mr. Chronos, you can now see why we believe that all three planets we attempt to deal with—our own Theon, Fantheon, and Earth are remarkably similar. Except, of course, in age. We all have water oceans, experience the same extremes in temperature, atmospheric pressures, and the force of gravity. We were all created from the same basic elements, we all grow similar foods, even admire the same things. For example, flowers. That last word is what this is all about. Flowers."

Chromos gasps. "It's about flowers? Your favor is about flowers? How can that be?"

"It's about The President of Fantheon himself, President Allister. Yes, President. He runs the whole planet. They no longer have separate countries. No need, they made war and hundreds of currencies obsolete a million years ago. This President was a horticulturist before he entered politics. He is, of course, still interested and is a member of a club that grows various flowers, such as hybridized orchids. Every year the club members submit exotic flowers the members have created and have grown themselves. He said he had heard that I had made a blue rose—probably the first. I told him exactly how to do it. I also told him no one will else will ever know. Did you know that, Chronos?"

"Know what? Did I miss a number? Must have dozed off. Sorry."

"About five years after the first phone call the President called me back and said he had won First Prize for new floral varieties that year with his "own" blue rose."

"And that is how I got the telescope. I am nice to them, they in turn are nice to me."

Chapter Ten

Perfection

**Planet Earth
Arlington Heights High school
Implanted Jack and Linda
The Year 2018**

We next arrive at a large high school with grades 10, 11 and 12. The students' ages ranged from 14 to 16 years old. The 16-year-old boys dripped with testosterone as they swaggered to class. The powerful hormone oozed out of every male pore.

In room 701, Miss Robert's Physics class was underway. One of her better students, Linda Grable, was delivering a ten minute presentation to this advanced class on the subject of vector calculus as an aid in solving probability calculations. Linda had worked very hard on the talk. Now almost at the end, she thought it had gone well. The school bell rang. Class was over. But for Linda, not quite over.

In many high schools there was often one Alpha male—handsome and super virile. Females the world over strongly responded to his presence. In one high school, years ago, his name was Van. He was the quarterback on the football team. His power over women was amazing. If Van was walking down the school hallway and a girl happened to be walking toward him and they both arrived at the same place at the same time, Van would look into her eye, say hello and her name and then her panties world fall off onto the hall floor.

As quick as a bolt of lightning he would snatch them up and eventually put them in his locker. It was said he had over 60 pair.

Jack Grable was football team captain and well-known high school stud horse—the super male in this high school. He leapt from his chair as quick as a gazelle and bolted to the front where Linda was making an exit through the classroom door. Jack reached her just in time. Linda stopped, turned, and looked at him.

Jack said, "That was an excellent presentation. I really liked it. I'm into math myself...I was wondering if we could meet, maybe tomorrow? There are several points you made that I would like to discuss with you."

Linda, still looking at him, replied "Okay. How about tomorrow after class? At the gym."

"Maybe just after three o'clock?" said Jack.

"Okay. See you tomorrow," said Linda.

As Jack was leaving the room, Miss Roberts called out from her desk, "Oh Linda, before you go could I see you for a few minutes?"

Linda smiled and began walking across the room toward the teacher's desk. "Sit down, dear. I just wanted to tell you that your talk was very impressive.

Remarkably advanced. Where and how did you learn all that math? And at such a young age?"

"Thank you so much, Mrs. English. Well, I have been interested in math ever since I was eight years old. I don't really know why. I have an uncle who knew about my interest and he bought me a four volume set called 'The World of Mathematics' published in 1995. I read all of them in one year. Ever since he has sent me two or three volumes from the Princeton Math series every year for Christmas. I think I now have ten of them...And oh, yes. I have read all the math books in our school library." She paused and said, "I just like the subject."

"Linda. Have you thought about college?" asked Mrs. English.

"Not really. We can't afford it," said Linda.

"Okay. Ever heard of Harvard University?"

"Sure, of course."

"Well, I know the faculty there quite well. There is a test they give to high school students. It is quite difficult. But if you pass it, it triggers a full scholarship. Completely free college for a four year degree. Remarkably, we already have someone in this school who has just passed it and has already locked up his scholarship."

Linda asked, "Who could that be?"

"If I tell you, it is very important that you not tell anyone else. Not even your mother. Not anyone. They might have you accused of collusion. It's Jack Foster. He has an IQ you would not believe."

Linda gasped, "Jack Foster, the football player? No way!"

"Believe it. He's the one. And oh, by the way, was that you I saw in the paper yesterday? Did you win the Regional High School Tennis Tournament?

"Yes ma'am. That was me."

The next day at the high school our virile young man sauntered down the halls of Arlington Heights High School on the way to meet a friend. Her name was Linda. He was supposed to meet her at three o'clock. He walked self-assuredly—wide stepped and head back. He was 16 years old and six feet two inches tall. He was Jack Foster, captain of the football team. People said he looked like a larger version of Brad Pitt.

He moved directly toward a group of girls. They pretended they didn't see him but they were all atwitter, some wringing their hands and about to swoon. Jack walked toward them, getting closer but still not looking at them. The halls were crowded. He almost bumped into Rebecca Swink who almost swooned. She opened her mouth to say hello but no sound came out. Jack walked on as if the girls were not there.

Just after three o'clock Linda was waiting by the doors to the gym. She was feeling anxious. Quite nervous. She could see Jack walking toward her from way down the hall. But her mind took her to early last night.

Linda's mind was at home.

Linda had been home in the kitchen helping her mom fix dinner. She was on her cell phone talking to her friend Cindy. Her mom listened to every word.

"Yeah. His name's Jack something...Captain of the football team. I don't think so...he does calculations. No way...seemed like a normal guy. He said he wanted to talk to me about probability theory."

Linda's mind was at school.

Linda saw the captain. He continued walking down the hall. No one else was around. He was walking toward her. He was much bigger than she remembered. Now he was looking directly at her.

Linda's mind was at home.

In her mind Linda saw herself in bed, reading. Her mother came to her bedroom door and hesitated. Linda, after a few moments, said, "Sure, Mom. Come in."

Her mother came in. She sat on the bed. "Linda dear, we need to talk a little, you have started your periods. And have started dating. Seeing boys. We need to talk."

"Mohhhhm". Linda dragged out the word.

"There are some things you may not be aware of. When you are out on a date with a young man are you aware of the risks you might have to deal with? Do you know what is going on in a young man's mind?"

Her mother was getting worked up no—more agitated. She was speaking loudly now. Then even louder. "There are things I things I have never told you about. Awful things." Her mother stopped and looked at the floor, tears in her eyes. "Some things boys might try. They might try even on your first date."

Linda asked "What earth are you talking about? Sex?"

"Of course. SEX!"

Linda's mind was at school.

Jack could see Linda pretty well. She was looking around. To her left. To her right. She turned all the way around. Odd. He thought she had seen him only few seconds ago. Jack continued forward.

Linda's mind was at home.

"Mom. I know young men want to have sex! All the girls know that! But the boys around here are okay. This is a good neighborhood. Such things do not happen here."

"A good neighborhood! Are you kidding? Do you really think that is all you need to be safe? What if he drinks alcohol? Sniffs cocaine? He will do whatever's necessary to get you in a compromising position. Then he will go crazy. Turn into an animal. It happens all the time. He will force you–"

"Mom! Enough! Stop!"

"Before you even know what is happening your clothes could be pulled off or torn aside and you would be penetrated. Then comes the eruption. He will scream like a maniac. His stuff in you. You could be raped!"

Linda's mind was at school.

A door opened just ahead and students poured out into the hall. Blocked, Jack stopped and waited. He could see Linda. She was fumbling with her books in her arms. He started running toward her.

Linda's mind was at home.

"Mom! Stop! No More!"

"I won't stop! It gets worse. If this happens you will likely be pregnant. Can you imagine? It will be all over the school. All over town! You will be scorned. The boy who did this will not take any responsibility. None. Ever. Your life could be ruined in one second."

Less than a few seconds passed before Linda seemed about to lose her balance and her books flew out of her hands. Jack was there and grabbed the books like a pro outfielder catches a long ball. No problem.

"Oh, thank goodness. Hi, Jack. There was a bee about to land in my hair. Thanks so much. Just in time."

Jack said "No problem, Linda. I'll carry them. How about we go over to the park across the street, you know, the one next to Jack in the Box."

"Perfect. Let's go."

Sitting on a park bench side by side, the two dabblers-in-math found amazing rapport. Both had had trouble with the concept of convergence of Fourier series, and both had enjoyed reading about the life story of the amazing 18th century Isaac Newton. Jack thought Linda's work on probability should and could be published.

Eventually Jack suggested they drive over to Mountain Mike's Pizza for dinner. Linda replied, "Great, let's go!" Off they went in Jack's ten year old Ford pickup truck.

During the next two weeks they saw each other almost every night. They went for walks in Linda's neighborhood. They would sit in canvas chairs in her backyard. It was May and warm every night.

Linda's mother would always keep an eye on them by peering through the kitchen window.

10th of August at 9:20 P.M. in Linda's back yard

Linda and Jack were sitting side by side in the backyard. There was no moon this night and the neighborhood had no street lights.

They would have usually parted company by now. Jack had a summer job with an architect who liked to start his day quite early.

Jack explained that if they waited until ten o'clock they could see something spectacular in the sky. "It's called the Perseid meteor shower. Starts about 30 minutes from now."

"Okay let's wait! I've never heard of it."

They were standing close together when streaks of light appeared in the dark sky.

Jack put his arms around Linda and they kissed. Both then experienced a massive transient shock wave moving through their bodies. They couldn't move. Hormones were released, flooding every organ, including the brain and the heart.

"Wow, what was that?" Jack looked at Linda. She had experienced the same thing. He began feeling a little dizzy. In his mind's eye, he saw Linda. *My God!* She was the most beautiful girl in the world. *Amazing!* How could he ever leave her? No way. He had to be with her forever. Starting now, he had to have her now. Now!

"Linda. I love you! Will you marry me? Be my wife?

"Yes! Of course! I love you too, with all my heart."

Peering out the kitchen widow, Linda's mom said, "Jesus Lord! What is going out there?" She snapped on an outside light.

Linda and Jack were in ecstasy, rolling around together on the backyard grass.

The implant from 16 years ago was still at work.

Chapter Eleven

Progress at Last

Planet Theon
Mother Nature
The Year 2018

Inside the great titanium and sapphire mansion built by Mother Nature, she herself was resting in her white snow leopard-covered recliner. She had set aside her 1015 power telescope and the new Vector 50 billion power listening device. Half asleep and day dreaming, she recalled a story she had once read. She visualized herself as the protagonist, with a bit of a twist, and let her imagination run wild while she conversed with a magic mirror.

'Mirror, mirror on the wall, who is the greatest geneticist of them all?'

'Why you are my dear, of course. Why do you ask?' answered the mirror in her mind.

"Well, because it has taken so damn long. And this human thing. It's still not finished," she muttered to herself. "We brought up the Homo sapiens 320,000 years ago and I thought we were done. But no. They are still not careful with whom and how they mate or 'pair-bond' as they call it. They still hook up with all kinds of low intelligence dummies. They haven't really improved themselves in the last 4,000 years. Yes, they create lots of new technology, but they still engage in devastating wars and tolerate millions living in abject poverty. We see seemingly never ending race problems and they even ignore mass shootings that occur in some countries almost daily."

"Perhaps worst of all, they are overpopulated and destroying their environment. The bottom line is that they are simply not smart enough to take care of themselves. So, we have been working on a new fix for this problem. I think we have done it. All we need to do now is to make things flow in a positive direction. We need to get more good mutations than bad ones so that bad genes completely disappear in time. Now we hope everything is going in the right direction and the problem will solve itself. We have finally found a way to get the better males linked with the stronger females. So, pretty soon the humans are going to be embedded with superstars. These people, the new leaders, will fix the problems themselves. Just wait and see. All you doubters. Just wait and see."

Several hours later

Mother Nature leaped out from under her thousand trillion power telescope and—running down a wide hall—shouted, "Atlas! Atlas! You are not going to believe this! We have done it! I just saw it. I heard it. We have created the next dominant species—Homo supierious. Atlas! Get over here. And bring some champagne!"

When Atlas arrived she said in an excited voice, "Just look at our super kid Jack Foster and the super female of the same age, Linda Grable! Our gene process functions like a charm. As this methodology runs over time, in a mere 300 years the new improved Homo sapiens will be on their way to populate the stars. Are you impressed?"

Atlas looked at her said, "I suppose so. It does look really good, but it doesn't prove the Y chromosome is stable enough that their children will pass the new genes onward."

"Yes, that's true, but we think it will."

"And what about doing this on our planet?"

"Atlas, everyone thinks we don't have a problem."

"Yeah, everyone but me. Any fool could see we are just as aggressive as anyone else." said Atlas.

"Well, we will see."

Chapter Twelve

Getting Old

**Back on Earth
The year 2021**

We continue our narrative in the small town of Clinton, Maine, population 3,406. In this town we find a large wood frame house on a quiet residential street. On a long stairway in this house, there is a man struggling to make his way to the second floor. The man's name is Dr. Robert Mann. This day, August 5, 2021, he has turned 81 years old.

The aging doctor was struggling because he was totally smashed, drunk as a boiled owl. He was not completely sure he was going to make it up the stairs and into his bedroom. He began shedding clothes about halfway up. The tie came off first and then his shoes. Reeling up the final steps, his blue blazer fell in a heap on the hall's hardwood floor. Seeing his bedroom, he staggered to it. He noticed his pajamas lay on the bed. Somehow, he managed to get them on. But he was asleep before his head came to rest on his pillow.

The night hours passed.

The first faint rays of sunlight were beginning to dance around the windows and walls in the good doctor's bedroom. It was still quite dark in the house.

Robert couldn't seem to get out of bed this August morning. He had a terrible headache and his ears were ringing. But it could have been worse. At least it was still summer time and the house was nice and warm—this a bit unusual for northern Maine where he had spent most of his early life. A place that could see minus 15°F in winter. For weeks on end.

It was now 5:30 A.M. in the morning. Robert had jumped out of bed and was racing in the dark to the bathroom. He had to pee. He really really had to pee. Almost there, but then he tripped on a boot he had carelessly left on the floor. Now, if only he could find a wall to touch and steady himself before he peed all over himself. But the wall wasn't there. Now he was falling. On his way down his foot was on the boot and it was somehow turning him around backwards. His pajama bottoms were quite loose and fell to his knees. He fell backwards on top of a junk-filled wastebasket he had not emptied in two weeks. His back hit the floor and urine shot straight up and then down onto his face and eyes. He pulled up his pajamas. Hot, wet and malodorous, he sat up and yelled with tremendous volume, "SHIT FUCK GODDAMN SON OF A BITCH!"

Two crows atop the house, busily engaged in the heady business of crow fertilization, were startled and took wing. A big dog down the way began barking.

Two hours later the doddering doctor had showered, donned some well-worn jeans and an old dark blue sweatshirt, placed his soiled pajamas in the washing machine, and cleaned up the mess on his bedroom floor. He was downstairs now in a leather recliner in his study, sipping the third mug of black coffee.

Robert thought to himself, 'Well, at least Katy didn't see that…but she knew that I simply cannot drink alcohol. She probably would have laughed. When was the last time I drank any alcohol? Must have been maybe five years ago, back when we landed our instruments on Titan…The guys drove me home to our rent house…Jesus.'

Two days passed.

That morning Robert lay in bed thinking about the party that had taken place downstairs that afternoon. His dear wife Katy was not there, of course, having succumbed to cancer two years earlier. His son had called from Los Angeles early in the day and had wished him well. Rufus, his dog, had looked at him the next morning with intensity and wagged his tail with special vigor.

He was thinking that it was remarkable that anyone here in Clinton had come over considering that most of the time over the last few years he had been out of town—either in Houston, Florida at the Cape, or in the Bay area working with Lockheed.

After breakfast, back in his recliner, a pile of mail and The Bangor Daily News lay on the floor next to his chair. He had picked up the newspaper and was starting to read an article about some of the large state parks an hour or two drive north from Clinton. He reread the glossy brochure saying 'We would like to welcome you to the wonderful Debsconeag Lakes Wilderness Area'.

"What the Hell. I'm going."

Two days later

Robert Mann was carefully and slowly driving his 10-year-old BMW down a narrow trail in a heavily wooded forest. He was looking for a nice spot to camp out in the woods. He was not interested in a cabin at some fancy resort. This time he longed for direct contact with nature. He was ready. He had brought his inflatable mattress and sleeping bag. He had food and water for two days. He just needed to find a nice spot and set up next to a big tree. Simple.

What about going to sleep? No problem. He had his flask of Jim Beam. Okay, but what if some wild animal came up sniffing him out in the night? Not likely. He had his camping spray to mask his human scent. But if an animal did come nosing around, they'd be in big trouble. He'd be on his back with a loaded 45 lying on his chest.

He stopped the car. He could see a steep hill about 200 feet from the road. He moved the car off the road and into the trees as far as he could. He collected his camping gear from the trunk of his car, crammed it all into his back pack and took off toward the hill. Coming quickly to a nicely cleared and flat area, he set up camp.

"Perfect", he said to himself.

Thirty minutes after dark, Dr. Robert Mann was asleep.

Almost ten hours later a little sunlight was making its way down through the trees. He looked up and saw a huge man at his feet.

The man began speaking to him. "Dr. Robert Mann? Is that you? This is amazing. We sent you a brochure about the area, but you found my camp? How on earth did you find me?"

"Find you? Your camp? Who are you?" asked Robert.

"You don't know? You've never had contact with Mother Nature? Do you remember back in 1960 at Sauers Harvest when you and Katy fell asleep at the table?"

"You mean 40 years ago?"

"Yes, 40 years ago. I was dressed as a waiter. I came to your table and offered you some complementary wine. It was drugged for near instant sleep. I walked behind you and gave you a dose of our gene cocktail. Used a hypodermic needle. It should have made you smarter, more intelligent."

"More intelligent? We did pretty well, but I don't recall any sudden improvements in my intelligence. I don't understand what this is all about. Who are you? What is all this about?"

"Okay, I can probably tell you everything now, but first you will have to promise and give me your word to not reveal any of what I am about to tell you, and not reveal this location. Not until I get some guidelines on how to proceed."

"Fine. I promise. I'm not sure I could find this location again even if I wanted to. And what is so special about this location?" asked Robert.

"You will see. The first thing you need to know is that I am not human." Steel removed his gloves and flexed his metal fingers. You can call me Steel."

"Far out."

"Pick up your gear and let's go inside." Steel walked over to the massive wooden door and moved it four feet to the left.

"Amazing. How did this door get here? This cave looks like it has been excavated."

"I did it myself. With that machine over there." Steel pointed to the nuclear excavator machine. "By the way, we have a bathroom designed for humans. We thought we might have human guests someday. You are the first."

"May I use it now?"

"Yes of course, take your time. It's there." Steel pointed to a wooden door. It was thirty minutes before Dr. Mann returned.

"You said 'we'. Are there others here?"

"Just the Flyer there. He can speak like me." "Okay. Tell me all about what you are doing here."

"Yes. Here is the story. I—we—came from planet Theon. It' s four light years from here. It took 100 years in space for me get here in the Flyer. The Flyer uses antigravity engines designed by engineers from a planet called Fantheon. It is said that Fantheon is at least one million years ahead of Theon in science and technology."

"There are three planets involved—Earth, Theon and Fantheon. From Theon, Earth is four light years distant and Fantheon is 15. Scientists on Theon noted centuries ago that their planet was almost identical to Earth. So, evolution was expected to take place essentially along the same path. Both planets evolved with a dominant species called Homo sapiens. On Theon it was concluded that a world government was created barely in time to prevent the countries from destroying themselves and their planet with the aggressive genus Homo sapiens in charge, who seemed determined to enter into a massively destructive nuclear war. Let me return to that in a few minutes, there are some other important parts of the story. Have you heard of the Greek gods who lived on Mount Olympus 1000 years ago?"

"Yes, what is this? Some kind of a dream? Am I going to wake up still my sleeping bag in a few minutes?"

"That's pretty clever. I would laugh but I don't know how. Not in my program," replied Steel.

"Laughing is easy you go, 'Ha ha ha'".

Steel tried, "Hah hah hah."

"Sorry, it doesn't sound genuine. Nothing is worse than a fake laugh."

"Okay, I don't know how to smile either."

"What about sex, can you have sex?"

"I hear people talk about it. I have not a clue."

"Then you don't need to worry about smiling or laughing."

"Excellent. I will continue explaining the situation with the three planets. I had mentioned the Greek gods. We have three people on Theon who claim they originated from these Greek gods. Their names are Mother Nature, Atlas, and Chronos. They claim they are around 1,000 years old and do not age. Mother Nature says she remembers an identical twin on planet Earth. Atlas is said to be very intelligent. Chronos is thought to be ridiculous and is ignored."

Dr. Mann listened, astonished at what he was hearing.

"Mother Nature is the main player in anything that might take place between you and me. She, despite her claims about her origin—which not everyone believes—is highly regarded as the most knowledgeable expert in the area of human genetics and DNA and she lectures in the universities. Mother Nature has been pushing me for many years to find a well respected person in order to find out what people think about a program designed to modify their values, attitudes and their intelligence in such a way that over time people in the world become opposed to war and less tolerant of things like the poor and homeless."

"Found anyone yet? " asked Robert.

"No. How about you?" asked Steel.

"You must be kidding. I am old, worn out, and not famous."

"I could fix that."

"And how could you do that?"

"Here is how. First, I'd give you a double dose of our gene enhancer. I did this once several years back and the guy turned into a genius and won the Nobel Prize in Physics. Then I pass on to you some major inventions that have been well received on other planets. You pass these on to industry and it won't be long before are you are famous. Then we set up some lectures to the public and see what they think about the changes that we think would be beneficial."

"Okay let's do it. At my age, what have I got to lose?" said Robert Mann.

A short time later Robert Mann woke up a new man. He looked and felt 20 years younger. His IQ had jumped 75 points.

Chapter Thirteen

THE BIG SELL

Dr. David Mann
After two new gene implants
The year 2025

Four years later, the big story that had the major TV news networks all aflutter concerned an older gentleman who had appeared on the scene quite suddenly, from almost total obscurity. This newcomer was now advising the President and several high-level Generals, and was giving speeches to the UN and big company CEOs such as Elon Musk, who still headed up Tesla. You couldn't turn on CNN or Fox News without a review of the latest unbelievable story about him. People claimed there was no subject he had not mastered.

News channels reported yesterday that Tesla had been given a description and working model of a new battery composed of electrodes of lithium and a magnesium alloy, all immersed in a liquid fluorocarbon. The inventor claimed higher cell voltages, more rapid recharging, and claimed it would not burn or ignite as today's lithium batteries sometimes do. The inventor claimed he held no patents covering this new technology.

They would be available to anyone who wanted use them for free.

Even more dramatic was his claim that his stem cell process would cure most cancers. Several hospitals had already reported that his process had been applied and had saved several terminally ill patients who were now miraculously cured.

The inventor's name was Dr. Robert Mann. In years past, he had consulted full time for NASA in their early years of outer space exploration and the development of their massive nuclear ICBM deployment.

Dr. Robert Mann
Speaks Tonight

It was Saturday night, and the Dallas Convention center had drawn 13,654 good Dallas citizens to hear and see the remarkable Dr. Robert Mann in person.

He walked onto the high stage and over to a microphone.

"Good evening ladies and gentleman. It is my pleasure to spend some time with you tonight focusing on what I believe is an important issue, yet it has received little attention."

"You have probably heard about my good fortune in coming up with an improved battery for the new wave of electric automobiles. And a new treatment for cancer. As you could imagine, I feel very fortunate to be able to contribute to society at such an advanced age."

"But tonight, I would like to present a controversial subject. As I mentioned, it's very likely you have not heard about it—probably not even thought about it. The subject relates to the question 'who exactly are we?' The answer might depend on who you ask—an anthropologist or a biologist? But let's be more specific on what we should tolerate, what we now allow and accept: seemingly never-ending war somewhere on the planet, and never-ending homelessness somewhere in the world. More generally, we live in a violent world. Perhaps you disagree. Consider the following: In the last century—that is, the years 1900 to 2000—there were about 150 million people killed in wars. Let's look at this on a daily scale. Here are some sobering statistics." Dr. Mann then clicked on a remote and a visual presentation appeared on a large screen behind him, displaying the following statistics:

Killed in wars world-wide in the last century: 4,000 per day

Killed in wars world-wide between 2000 to 2018: 3,000 per day

Violent crime in the US in 2019: 3,300 per day

"A person might argue that the United States cannot prevent these things. They are often beyond our control. But to allow or ignore the following—is this who we really are? Let's look at a few more numbers."

1. Today, in the United States, we have 580,000 homeless citizens.

2. In the world today, there are 150 million homeless.

3. About 700 million people in the world go to bed hungry.

4. The U.S. enters into a new war about every 20 to 25 years. This has resulted in about two million deaths.

5. Since about 1800 the world has lost 1/3 of its forests.

6. According to International "The News", Jan 8, 2020, The US has been at war 225 out of 243 years since 1776.

Mann then returned to his prepared speech. "I must ask again, who are we? Maybe Anthropology will tell us. Assuming we begin with Australopithecus, an ape-like early human, the human race had been evolving for three million years in the form of tribes. The tribes gradually assumed common physical, if not mental characteristics. The utility of the tribe was that it advanced the success of procreation. The tribe had a far greater success of survival than humans living alone or in pairs. Food was obtained via a process called hunting and gathering."

"Over the 2.5 million years of our tribal evolution, we could have gone through as many as 150,000 generations. We eventually appeared as Homo sapiens. And, we most likely killed all the various human species until we got back to the apes who, of course, didn't threaten us."

"Some division of labor appeared. The men evolved mental and physical skills leading to greater success in the hunt and gained enhancements for defense against competing and attacking tribes. The women enhanced their success at raising children, preparing food and attracting males. The beneficial traits were passed on."

"Those perceived as beautiful were also more likely to be healthier, freer of infection, freer of birth defects, perhaps even stronger. Mate selection thus included beauty. This gradually created the perception of race for widely scattered human groups. Again, those details which characterize various human groups that were thought to be favorable were coded into our genes and were passed on and could also generate the human tendency for prejudice."

"Some 10,000 years ago, human tribes began to join together and cities were formed. Various technical advances appeared—such as farming, language, advances in weaponry and finally the sciences, industry and medicine. Natural selection through survival of the fittest was no longer operating strongly, and evolutionary changes in humans slowed. But evolution never completely ceases. Some additional human characteristics may be undesirable, yet not now obvious to us."

A large man with snow white hair grabbed a microphone from an attendant and in a loud voice said "Now wait just a minute here! We didn't come from no apes. God created man after his own image. And in your words, only the beautiful are free of infection, and free of birth defects. You're out of your mind!"

"Sir, you have a good point. I have ignored religion. But let me clear up one point you made about beauty. You just said that I said that only the beautiful are free of infection and free of birth defects. That, of course, is not true and not what I said. My statement was "those perceived as beautiful were more likely to be healthier, freer of infection, freer of birth defects, perhaps even stronger." Please note I said freer not free. This could mean a slight difference or a large difference. Several studies have shown this trend to be true. You made a point about God and evolution. Not to worry about evolving from an ape. We have all evolved through a very long and tortuous process here on Planet Earth. This is known from a vast fossil record now dated and organized in the 200-year field of Paleontology. The earliest life forms we know of were microscopic organisms (microbes) that left traces of their presence in rocks about 3.7 billion years ago. The first fish appeared around 530 million years ago. The first true vertebrate—an animal with a backbone—then appeared with an enormous variety of species."

Dr. Mann paused, noted that the audience was listening, took a breath and continued. "Approximately 20 million years ago, during the Triassic Period, the dinosaurs appeared, evolved from early reptiles. From Australopithecus five million years ago we finally arrived at Homo sapiens. This is what the fossil record reveals. Perhaps God was responsible for all of it."

Mann then looked at the man who had spoken and remarked "Sir. Let me ask you to consider this. Do you think God would be pleased if we stopped killing millions in wars and took care of 159 million homeless? We cannot be 100% sure we can do that, but we would like to try."

He continued "Today there exists a technology called gene editing. By inserting certain genes into a person's bloodstream, the existing genes can be improved or changed. For example, a person could be made smarter or less smart, more or less aggressive, more or less empathetic and so on. Let's take a look at Biology."

"Who are we? Biology will tell us. In all living things a chemical structure exists that defines not only what the thing is, but also how it is made. It defines where all the parts go, how they are encoded and in what order they are to be made. It defines what basic chemical elements are needed for construction, for the beings' ultimate size, how it will produce energy, if it is to move, how long it will live, how it will deal with waste, what will be used to cover its body, such as thick hair, skin, scales or feathers and the exact locations where everything must finally reside. It must define the oxygen entry and the oxygen system in the body and exactly how it is processed, either with lungs, gills, or moving in sap."

"How could all the above information be stored? A computer could perhaps use computer programs and input ones and zeros, an engineer might use writing in a specified language and drawings on paper. Nature does in all with DNA, a molecule shaped like a double helix or two spirals linked together with two chemical units called bases. There are four types of bases which can be selected in different combinations—forming a code."

"DNA, or deoxyribonucleic acid, is the most important molecule in all of Biology. It defines who and what we are. It makes the enzymes that power many chemical reactions and the hemoglobin that carries oxygen in the blood. Inside our cells at least 20,000 different proteins are produced, making you what you are. It creates the complex muscle and nerve cells in your body. Our DNA contains the genetic code necessary to produce RNA molecules, which in turn produce proteins used all over the body."

Mann then clicked the next illustration onto the large screen. It read:

Today's hot new subject in Biology: Gene Editing

"Gene editing is performed using enzymes, particular ones have been engineered to target a specific DNA sequence, where they introduce cuts into the DNA strands, enabling the removal of existing DNA and the insertion of replacement DNA. Could we use gene editing to solve the problem presented here?" he queried the audience. "We could!" he answered excitedly. "In the creation of our children. We might choose to modify only two human characteristics, aggressive behavior and intelligence. Let's explore these two traits."

The next image on the large screen read as follows:

1. Aggressive behavior. In the Journal of Molecular Psychiatry, a paper was published in 2018 stating that 40 genes had been found to be related to aggressive behavior in humans and mice.

A murmur went through the audience and then the next image came up. It read:

2. Intelligence. There is no one IQ gene, but one study, published in Nature Genetics, found evidence precise enough to determine that there are at least 22 specific genes related to intelligence. Which led to a key statistic: together, these 22 genes accounted for about 5% of the differences in intelligence scores.

Dr. Mann then said, "I'd like to explain more about this concept of editing chromosomes." He went on to explain, "In the nucleus of each cell, the DNA molecules are packaged into thread-like structures called chromosomes. Each chromosome is made up of DNA tightly coiled many times around proteins called histones that support its structure. The Y-chromosome is inherited more or less unchanged from father to son to grandson, indefinitely. Chromosomes contain the DNA that determines our inherited characteristics, and the Y-chromosome is one of the 46 chromosomes in the nucleus of each of the cells of all human males. Most chromosomes, including the two X-chromosomes possessed by females, get recombined or shuffled each generation before being passed down to offspring. But the Y-chromosome is unique in remaining more or less unchanged when passed from father to son."

"Each person normally has one pair of sex chromosomes in each cell. The Y-chromosome is present in males, who have one X and one Y-chromosome, while females have two X-chromosomes."

"If we placed our edited genes in the Y-chromosomes they would be passed on indefinitely until the entire population was modified. This would include new technologies for enhanced long-term stability of the modified Y-chromosome."

Mann paused for a moment, wondering how the audience was reacting to this information. He then looked toward the white haired man and said, "Sir, back to your question. Let me pose the question I asked before once again. Do you think God would be pleased if we stopped killing millions in wars, and took care of 159 million homeless? We cannot be 100% sure we can do that this way, but we would like to try."

"Again, there exists today a new and growing technology—gene modification. By inserting certain genes into a person's bloodstream, existing genes can be improved or changed. For example, a person could be made smarter or less smart, more or less aggressive, more or less empathetic and so on. This technology is still in its early stages. The question is: should we continue the work?"

The next slide read:

1. People can be made substantially smarter with large increases in IQ. This should generate economic improvements.

2. Those with greater empathy might find war absolutely intolerable

3. We also might find people in situations of hunger intolerable to the rest of the world."

"If we were less aggressive, this could also reduce the chance of support of war, if not the elimination of war itself. We might solve the problems of war and of the homeless by changing the importance of only three human values: intelligence, empathy, and aggressiveness."

"Please take ten minutes to discuss this among yourselves. I will return shortly and ask for a show of hands for or against continuing the research."

The first mistake Robert made that evening was not realizing that strong political positions were already in place in this part of the country. The positions of most of the population in such an area as Dallas, Texas regarding such a large government program were quite predictable. A vote for any new large Government program would be close to 100 % no.

The second mistake made by Dr. Mann this day was far more serious. Indeed, catastrophic. He had brought Steel to the meeting. Steel had been sitting quietly with several others on the stage. And Steel's perception of the talk was that the audience loved Dr. Mann. And that they loved what they were hearing. In reality, Mann had put 95% of the audience to sleep.

Steel however, was completely convinced that of course they would vote to proceed with the new research. Then he began to think more complex thoughts, albeit erroneous thoughts. He interpreted the audience's silence as approval. He then thought that when they learned that the work had actually started 115 years ago and that it was going very well and many people had already greatly benefited **and that he himself was the one who gave them the new genes that he would be a national hero. No longer would he have to hide the fact that he was not human. They would love him for who he actually was.** *Of course they would! 'What am I waiting for?'* roared through his mind, if it could be called a mind.

No more hiding!

They are going to love me!

With no warning, Steel rose from his chair and walked to the microphone. "Ladies and gentlemen, my name is Franklin Steel. Dr. Mann's story seems to be pleasing you. I can tell you this much, when the time comes there could be many more people here like me to distribute the new genes."

A man in the third row had grabbed a portable microphone from a nearby usher, "Sir. Excuse me, Sir. What do to you mean by people like me?"

Steel thought a minute and said, "Well, let me explain first that I probably shouldn't use the word 'people'. I am an actually an android. I am almost completely inorganic. Let me show you." Steel grabbed his heavy long sleeve shirt and lifted it up over his head and laid it on the table. And there he was. His surface not skin but hundreds of polished blocks of stainless steel, now shimmering in the Convention Center lights like a bejeweled ancient Egyptian pharaoh. Steel then bounded down the aisle to a railing and jumped 20 feet like some sort of giant insect down to the main floor and headed toward the man who had asked the question.

The man who asked the question yelled, "What the fuck!" fell over backward, then jumped back up and ran off as fast as he could.

The first three rows of people were in panic. Women were screaming. Men were leaping and running. Some fell or were knocked down and were scrambling on their knees. In seconds, the whole theater was in an uproar.

Steel stopped his advance, seemingly puzzled by what was happening. Three large men in dark suits arrived with guns out and pointed at Steel. They moved slowly toward him. Steel, still bewildered, spoke loudly at the gunmen, "Hey guys what is the problem? I am not here to hurt anyone!"

The men encircled him. Quick as a bolt of lightning, Steel took one gun away from the person standing closest and was about to snatch a second weapon when the man pulled firing a .45 caliber hard steel-alloy slug directly at Steel's chest.

Like a sledge hammer blow and almost penetrated, this instantly triggered a complete change in Steel's AI processing and actions. New faster acting circuits were switched on—the survival program was activated and the old Steel was turned off. He was then in the threat and survival mode. The limitation that made him incapable of injuring a human was switched off.

He would not remember his actions during the next few minutes.

Steel lunged toward the man who had fired, his energy source at its max, snatched his gun from him and with a second motion—fueled as though energized by a jet engine—struck him in the head with his arm. The man's head ripped from his body and became airborne, the thing headed for the balcony. A wide-eyed and already shrieking overweight woman dressed in white could see it streaking directly towards her. The head landed near her feet splattering blood on her and anyone else sitting close by. She and her husband and everyone else within several seats scrambled away from the awful thing as if it were radioactive and about to explode.

Steel had the third man—who had been reaching for something in his jacket—by the feet and was twirling him around in the air. He let him go down close to the floor and he slid across the marble floor like a snowboarder down a steep mountain until he slammed into a wall about 100 feet away.

Steel stood in place vibrating and buzzing with jets of howling white steam blowing off excess energy.

Downstairs, Robert Mann, who had been in the men's room, raced up to Steel and shouted, "Let's go! To the Flyer. Now!" They both took off running.

"We need to go to Commerce Street onto the Commerce Bridge. But should we really be in a hurry?" asked Steel, not sure why they were running.

Mann explained, "Yes! The police are undoubtedly looking for you. For us."

Steel replied, "I know how to speed this up. I'll get down on my knees. You get on my back. Put your arms around my neck and I'll run."

Moments later Steel and Robert Mann were moving on dark side streets at 45 miles per hour toward the Trinity River. Fifteen minutes later they stepped into the Flyer.

"Let's go up to your secret spot in Maine. Disappear for a while. How long will that take?"

"About one hour," said Steel. In exactly an hour they had settled in their State of Maine woodsy hideout. After settling and making sure they had not been observed Dr. Mann began to finally relax. He sat across from Steel and said,

"By the way, I'd like hear about any situations you are dealing with or know about, that I don't. All surprises are bad."

"There is one thing you probably should know about. I don't think Mother Nature knows about it either. Atlas has probably figured it out," said Steel.

"Okay, what?"

"I overheard a conversion only few days after I was built. I don't think I was supposed to hear it. A Theon engineer had been working on me with a Fantheon engineer all day long and they had been using a communication line the whole time. The man from Theon said he would be back in a few minutes. He left the line open. Then I could hear a conversation in the background. Some Fantheon engineers were talking about 50 space ships that had just left for Theon. They said it was going take 375 years to get to Theon. That was 215 years ago. So, they should arrive 160 years from now."

"About 50 space ships? That is incredible! Why were they doing that?" asked Dr. Mann.

"I don't know, at that point they stopped talking," said Steel.

"Shouldn't you tell someone at Theon about this? Perhaps someone very intelligent who would know what to do," said Mann.

"Yes, of course. I know who would be perfect. Hey, my good friend Rocket, how about setting up a call for me?"

"Sure," Rocket replied. "To whom?"

"A man called Atlas, he lives in the same house as Mother Nature."

"Okay. I will see what I can do," replied Rocket.

Ten minutes later Rocket had made the connection.

"Who the fuck wants me at 2:30 in the morning?" said Atlas as he heard the phone ring.

"Sir, there will be five minutes delay in each direction."

"Yeah. Yeah. I know, operator. I will wait," said Atlas.

"Hello Mr. Atlas. This is Steel. I am the android that your friend Mother Nature has been talking to for the past 150 plus years. I have been injecting the gene altering material into the people here on Earth for the past 50 years. I am currently working here on Earth with a Dr. Robert Mann. He has suggested that I inform you about a conversation I happened to overhear during my assembly in the year 1810."

"Fine, this better be good," said Atlas.

"Some Fantheon engineers were talking about 50 space ships that had just left for Theon. They said it was going to take 375 years to get to Theon. That was 215 years ago. So, they should arrive 160 years from now. I didn't hear anything about the purpose of this mission or the size or type of spacecraft. And please tell Mother Nature that Dr. Mann gave a talk about gene substitution in Dallas. It did not go well. We didn't learn anything about the people's attitude about the technology."

About ten minutes later Steel received the following short message:

"Thank you for the information about the space craft from Fantheon."

Chapter Fourteen

The Peril

Capital City
2025
The Presidential Palace

President Freeman, the president of Theon, was speaking. "I have called this meeting to discuss a possibly serious situation between us and the Planet Fantheon. For the record those now present are Vice President Adams, Secretary of State Russell, Secretary of Defense Cole, General Lorenz, Major Morris, and Atlas. Mother Nature will join us shortly. And some may know, she is the owner of a remarkable telescope designed for her by the Fantheons. That telescope could possibly help resolve this matter. Alright, Atlas, tell us what you've heard from Earth."

"Some of you may be aware of my colleague Mother Nature's interest in Planet Earth. This is partly driven by her unique capability to closely observe the planet with the remarkably powerful telescope obtained from Fantheon. In any case, back around the year 1800 our government was very concerned about the basic nature of the current human species Homo sapiens. Many scientists concluded that this species was inherently far too aggressive and would be always at war somewhere on the planet. This was the main driving force for the creation of our world government, which as we know solved the problem."

"An alternative solution was gene modification toward a less aggressive and more intelligent species. The necessary gene implants were prepared. We then manufactured and sent an android we called Steel to Earth. He left Theon back in 1810. He arrived on Earth 100 years later in 1910 and proceeded to implant a number of young people. But we had to wait some 50 years to determine if the procedure actually worked and didn't cause any harmful side effects. It did not. It now appears to be quite successful, so we've injected approximately 400 more people. However, this is not enough, of course, to turn the war problem around quickly enough. During this entire period Steel had been directed by Mother Nature."

President Freeman stood, cleared his throat and said, "Mr. Atlas, l realize it is rude to interrupt your presentation, but there is some relevant information about you that I think the other members of this meeting should be aware of. 200 years ago someone put up an orbiting telescope, focused on deep space. They saw flashes of light that were attributed to all-out nuclear war on the populated planets. It was seen as yet another example that Homo sapiens are too aggressive to survive. It must have been some 50 years later that you, Mr. Atlas, made a detailed mathematical analysis that showed the streaks of light are never explosions at ground level. To the contrary, they were all more than 100,000 meters from the surface. They were celebrating disarmament. This was major help toward our own successful disarmament and our World Government established now years ago."

This triggered applause from the group.

"Thank you, Mr. President I appreciate your input. However, let's get back to the issues of today," Atlas continued. "Recently Steel has been working with a famous inventor and technology expert, a Dr. Robert Mann. It was Mann who received the following statement from Steel. Steel had heard it when he was here being prepared for his journey to Earth. Here is what he said. I have it recorded."

He pushed a remote and a scratchy recording began to play. Some Fantheon engineers were talking about 50 space ships that had just left for Theon. They said it was going take 375 years to get to Theon. That was 215 years ago. So, they should arrive 160 years from now.

"I didn't hear anything about the purpose of this mission or the size or type of spacecraft," Atlas added.

"So, 50 space ships are on their way. That might mean as many as 5,000 Mr. Steels. Could this be an invasion?" asked normally taciturn Vice President Adams.

"An invasion? What are you talking about?" shouted President Freeman, the room now all abuzz.

"Sir, I have been pondering about Planet Fantheon for years. Why are they so kind to us? Who are they? Are they human flesh and blood or are they all some version of Mr. Steel?" said Atlas.

"We don't even know if they are human or not?" asked the President.

"Not really," replied Atlas.

"Mr. Atlas, I have a question for you. These 50 spacecraft—if they were flying in close formation could they be seen with your telescope?" asked General Lorenz.

"Only if you knew the exact coordinates of their location, sir. Otherwise, it would be a hopeless task trying to find them, until they were much closer," said Atlas.

"But still—if they were planning an attack, it would make sense for them to be widely separated in case we were to send missiles up to destroy them," said General Loren.

"Yes, that makes sense, sir," said Atlas.

The President directed a question to Secretary of Defense Cole. "Have we still got any nuclear weapons?"

"I don't think so," responded Cole. "The disarmament of 2012 essentially destroyed all the nuclear weapons in the entire world. But if we have to, we can make more. We apparently have 100 years to do it."

The door to the conference flew open and in strolled Mother Nature with two of the President's aids.

"Hello gentlemen. I'm sorry to be late but I have wonderful news. Some helpers from Fantheon are going to arrive here in few days and build us a science museum for the many projects they have helped us with. We–"

The President interrupted her and blurted out, "A few days! Are you serious? We are going to face an armada from space!"

"Armada? Where did that come from? According to President Wickets, he is sending us 15 Mr. Steel type helpers in–"

"In how many space craft?" interrupted Atlas.

"Five vessels, so what?" said Mother Nature.

"How big?" asked Atlas.

"How big? You tell me. I got the coordinates and took pictures with the telescope," said Mother Nature. She brought out a device from her pocket and projected an image on a blank wall. The image showed five vessels only a few feet apart.

The President turns to Alas and asked, "Mr. Atlas this is completely contrary to what Steel said he had heard and then brought to you. Can you explain?"

"There are two discrepancies. The number of spacecraft and the total flight time from Fantheon to Theon," said Atlas.

"The President told me that flight times for non-living objects had been improved so that now Flyers could move through space at 7% the speed of light. The number back when you sent our android Steel to Earth was 4% of the speed of light."

"So, for all practical purposes they are already here. Hear any explosions outside in the distance?" said Mother Nature.

Atlas sprang from his chair and crossed the room like a bolt of lightning and slammed the door on his way out with loud bang.

Loadstone and Iron

The meeting room emptied quickly, leaving only the President and Mother Nature. President Freeman leaned back in his chair just for a few seconds and let the stress flow out of his body.

The President looked up and saw a beautiful female staring back at him. Then he said, "Miss Nature that was quite a performance. You stopped a possible chain of events dead in its tracks, which otherwise could have been absolutely catastrophic. I admit I had heard good things about you. I must apologize for not having formally invited you into the government."

"Thank you, Mr. President, but you need not apologize, you are still new to your office. I am so sorry to have heard about your wife's passing early last year."

"Yes, my wife's illness was terrible. but for today let me invite you to share glass of wine with me and let this day come to a peaceful close," said the President.

She nodded. He took her hand and out the door and down a hall they began walking. Mother Nature's thoughts suddenly shifted gear. 'I am now walking with a very handsome man in his mid 40s to exactly where I do not know.'

President Freeman said, "They've recently finished a beautiful suite of rooms for me close by, just down the hall. It has a magnificent view of the harbor. Here we are."

He opened the door and they both went in.

The President pulled out a cell phone and said, "Henry, bring up some wine and two glasses and maybe something to eat. I am in the new suite. Miss Nature, look out of this window. The view is relaxing," Freeman suggested.

She sat down on a deep cushioned couch. The view was quite nice: blue water and sky, fishing boats, circling sea birds. The President joined her on the couch. The door opened and Henry rolled in a cabinet and table with wine and shrimp with a red sauce nearby.

The President poured the wine and handed it to his new lady friend. "Miss Nature, we should probably forget about all this for a while and simply relax, but I have a question I feel I must ask. Then I promise we'll rest and maybe just contemplate the harbor."

"Go ahead. My day hasn't been that tiring."

"Alright. Good. The question is about the gene implants on planet Earth. What exactly were we trying to do. How did it go?"

"Do you know what a gene is?" she asked.

"Sort of. They are little pieces from our DNA that make up our heredity."

"That is true. But we humans have perhaps 50,000 genes. They have many other functions. They carry coded information from our DNA to make proteins. They make repairs following injury. Moreover, they make body parts in the correct order at the correct location as we grow to full grown. And they determine various attributes which as you mentioned, we pick up from our parents—eye color, height, various details of our facial structure, and our hair texture and color. But also more subtle attributes such as intelligence, agelessness, empathy, and even honesty. We believe that in time—that is, after many centuries, virtually the entire world's population will be compelled to always tell the truth."

"Wow. That is impressive. And it fits the need. As the problem was related to me, we believe that our species Homo sapiens is too aggressive and will eventually destroy itself in an all-out nuclear war. So, we authorized you some many years ago to see if gene editing could fix that problem."

"That is true, I have my own lab with a staff of four biologists. I had been working on the problem for 50 years. We were ready to go in the year 1810. We sent Steel to Earth to get started."

"That is amazing."

"For the implant, we have 60 new genes and about 90 that will replace some already there. The implanted genes are dominant so with time we should have altered eight to ten billion people on Earth in about 300 years. So far it seems to be working"

"And you are able to monitor their behavior with a telescope you got from Fantheon?"

"Yes, I have seen some amazing results. But of course, not on the whole planet."

"That is an amazing story. You should be very proud." The President paused and then said, "Now we can really wind down. Let's just sit here for a while without talking."

"Wonderful idea," she said as she leaned back into the cushion.

Henry, the waiter, backed out and left without saying a word.

A half-hour later the lady reached over and ran her fingertip carefully under the President's left eye. She then held up her figure up and proudly announced "Testosterone leaking out."

Then suddenly she put her hands over her eyes and leaned down and sobbed, "What am I doing? Leading you on? To where?"

"Miss Nature. What's wrong? You don't have to do anything you are not comfortable with. Please do not worry. I know life can get complicated. You can tell me anything."

"First, I must apologize for my behavior during the past few minutes. I cannot go with to you your bedroom and have sex—not that it would be wrong. I have a problem. And if tell you what it is, you will probably find it impossible to believe. I can barely believe it myself."

"Tell me. I know you are hurting, Tell me and maybe you will feel relieved," said the President.

"All right, here it is. Again, you don't really have to believe it. I was born on Earth in the year 961."

"I don't mean to interrupt, but that was over 1,000 years ago!"

"Yes, it was. I was nine years old. An android from Fantheon snatched me off the street and took me to his Flyer and traveled across space for 350 years to Fantheon. On the way they applied their incredible advanced technology to me. They somehow implanted into my brain an advanced and detailed knowledge of Biology. They made me into a new person who was 35 years old. Then I traveled to Theon and knew the language when I arrived. That is now 750 years total. I woke up on our wharf area down where we were just were looking."

Freeman listened, stunned.

"I was age nine years old speaking Italian. Then I found myself on a planet I had never heard of, with a new body, and somehow speaking a language I'd never heard of. You cannot imagine the shock! It was terrible. The year was 1720. Atlas had the same experience in a different Flyer, at the same time as my journey. There's more. It gets worse. Much worse."

The President was speechless.

"I have studied my DNA. It has been modified! If I have a child it will not be human. I don't really know what it will be. But it will be aggressive. And ugly. A monster. There is no way I can risk such a thing happening."

She leaned back on the couch, emotionally drained.

The President did not speak for a few minutes. But then he said. "That is so sad. Such a thing to live with. It doesn't matter if I believe it or not. I know you do. I will honor that. I will never repeat the story to anyone. Let me get someone to drive you home."

Chapter Fifteen

The Workers Arrive

President Freeman sat in his spacious office overlooking the sparkling water of the harbor. He had been busy. He had assigned Secretary of State George Russell to make the arrangements for the arrival of the five space ships from Fantheon. He had also suggested that Russell keep Atlas by his side during the several weeks.

"They appear to be only one day away and Atlas has made radio contact." Freeman told Russell.

Russell's phone rang, jolting him out of his reverie. "Yes, Hello. This is secretary of State George Russell. To whom am I speaking?"

"Hello, Mr. Secretary. This is Mr. Volt. I am in charge of our 15-worker crew. The only information we need right away is where we should first set down on your planet."

"Yes of course. On the north side of this city, we have a large vacant space that should work. It is bordered by a river on the north, a large freeway on the south and an airport on the east. We can have a truck there with a sign on top that reads 'HERE'," explained Russell.

"That sounds very good, Mr. Russell. We will arrive at approximately 1:30 P.M.," said Volt.

"Okay, we are looking forward to a fine relationship. In that regard would you like to take some time looking around the city before starting the project?" asked Russell.

"No, sir. We would prefer starting as soon as possible. In that regard, we would like your help as soon as we arrive. We would like to go straight to a bank. There we will deposit the 900 pounds of gold we brought with us. We understand you are familiar with the risks. We'll need the provision of a truck to transport the gold. I would then need four credit cards to use against these funds. The names on the cards are to be Volt, Push, Gene and Iron. The following day we would appreciate the delivery of three large automobiles and one bus that would accommodate 15. We can pay for these vehicles with the cards. You may select the makers of the vehicles."

"Mr. Volt, we appreciate your enthusiasm, but it might be better for you to select the vehicles yourselves a bit later. You will first require getting drivers' licenses and establishing an address. We will, of course, assist all of you in this process. These activities could be a good way for you and your crew to get acquainted with our ways of doing business. But I do agree that we should move your gold into a bank as soon as possible. So, I will have a truck there to transport the gold. Also, if we have time, I would like to drive around the city and show you some of the possible locations for the museum. We are wondering what sort of building you had in mind. Even a medium-size museum could cost around 10 to 20 times more than the 900 pounds of gold you're bringing. But that does not consider the fact that you are going to provide the labor which, of course, is a large fraction of the total cost," said Russell.

"Alright, sir, we understand. But I would like to show you our drawings tomorrow. Then we can began our detailed planning, Until tomorrow, Mr. Russell." *Click.* Volt disconnected the call.

Atlas, who had been reclining in a lounge chair, listening to the call, said, "Wow! That was really something. These guys want to start immediately. Before we know where to build it, what it will look like, what it will cost, who pays for it, how large it will be—before the site is even cleared, before we have detailed architectural drawings approved by the city and the President and so on?" said Atlas.

"And our man Volt has the social skills of what?" asked the Secretary.

"How about an alligator?" replied Atlas. "Yeah. I was thinking more along the lines of some type of excrement," said the Secretary with a smile.

"Right! But, wait, I have an idea." said Atlas. "Maybe we could interest them into playing professional sports until we are ready to start the museum. Which could easily be a year or more away. Mother Nature persuaded many countries here some sixty years ago to play basketball and baseball. These sports are now played all over the world," said Atlas.

"Alright my man, see if they are interested," replied Secretary Russell.

"Probably be a couple days from now before that might work. Or more."

The Planning Stage

During the following ten days rapid progress was made. From the one drawing presented by the androids which was a well done facade, it was concluded that what Fantheon had in mind was a building of modest size. The group quickly located a downtown building which in total occupied one half city block. The building was in a fairly affluent section of downtown. But it was quite old and obsolete, so no one would miss it. It was thought a two-story underground parking garage would accommodate about 400 cars. The old building was already for sale at a modest price. It was also decided to proceed with the front facade as presented by Mr. Volt. The next day they were told that all this information had been sent to Fantheon. Secretary Russell and the others were told that the Fantheon people were very pleased with everything and to proceed with the project. However, the next thing done by Atlas and the Secretary was almost a big mistake. They needed to tread lightly.

It was an early September morning when Atlas drove out to see Volt and the crew.

He pulled his car into the site and parked. There they were, all fifteen, sitting on the ground staring at a fire they had made, apparently by pulling a tree out of the ground and pulling it apart with their steel hands. Burning slowly, it did produce a rather pleasant camp fire.

"Mr. Volt, may I have the attention of your crew for a few minutes?" asked Atlas politely.

"Of course." Fourteen heads turned simultaneously to face Atlas.

"Okay. As you are aware, it is going to be quite some time before we can start the labor intensive work on the museum building itself. First, we must execute highly detailed drawings for everything—the interior and exterior of all surfaces, halls, doors, ceilings, rooms, lighting, plumbing and other utilities and, of course, the overall layout and organization. We must design the exhibit rooms, auditoriums, offices, the landscape, and the parking garage. We have to detail all exterior facades, bathrooms, kitchens and maintenance areas. Everything must be checked for building codes. All material and labor costs must be listed. The financial and investment issues must be completed and settled. Building permits must be issued. The existing building must be demolished and the rubble hauled away. The basement must be excavated, as we have decided to build a two-story deep car garage there which we believe could provide parking space for 400 cars. These last two tasks are executed, of course, by heavy machines and trucks. All of this must be complete before we begin the labor-intensive work of constructing the museum itself. We have been told that you are highly skilled in this area. We are honored for your help in this area."

Volt rose from his place on the ground and said, "Thank you, Mr. Atlas, for the detailed scenario of building the museum. Such details are remarkable in their similarity to construction practices at our home planet. Indeed we 15 could take care everything you mentioned. We have built three museums over the past 35 years. You would need hire no one except workers for excavation and hauling away of the debris."

Atlas heard a break in the dialogue and said, "Mr. Volt, that is truly impressive. Just perfect! But in the meantime let me introduce you to...baseball!" He looked at the sitting group. "You are soon going to be famous! Here is what we could do. We could teach you how to play baseball. We'll tell everyone, the media and baseball team owners, that we would like to play some demonstration games with a professional baseball team. You could say that you started playing some games at home—that is, Fantheon—and you think you are good enough to win some games here. Say that you arrived here a week ago and it took 214 years to get here in five spacecraft. You could say 'As I'm sure you have heard we are androids. We are made of steel, motors, bearings, a power supply and electronic controls. But we are not robots. We are completely autonomous. No one operates us but ourselves. Our speed and strength are the same as a reasonably successful male athlete's. If we win a game, it will be due to luck or high levels of skill. Finally, we are not dangerous. We will avoid running player to player collisions.' "

"I assume you are going to teach us how to play." said Mr. Iron.

"Of course," said Atlas. "Let's start now. Let me briefly define the game. Then everyone can watch a video. I've brought a big screen TV, a nice video explaining the game, and some advice on how to win. Tomorrow morning, I'll come back with a bus. We can practice at a large stadium where the professionals play."

"One more thing. You'll need uniforms. I'm going to get uniforms for everyone. So, Mr. Volt please give me a list of names for all 15 of you. Use the Theon alphabet of course. The uniform will include the name of your team on the front and the player's name on the back. How about 'Astronauts'? Also, each player will have a number from 1 to 15. Each of you select a number. They will appear on the front and back. You will also wear caps. They will have the team name on them. 'Astronauts', okay?

Atlas said, "Let me explain the basics of the game before you watch the video. Baseball is a game played with a wooden bat, a three inch round ball, and leather gloves. It's played between two teams of nine players on a field with four white bases laid out into a diamond shape—a square oriented so that its diagonal line is vertical."

"The bat is round and just under three inches in diameter. A player, called the pitcher, stands in the center of the diamond and from about 60 feet away he throws the ball toward a player on the opposite team who holds the bat. The thrown ball must be within a strike zone, near the batter, or the batter doesn't have to try to hit the ball. The batter tries to hit the ball into the field in such way that players on the other team will fail to catch it before it hits the ground. If it does hit the ground, they will retrieve it and throw it to the base where a player on their team catches it and touches the player or the base before the batter gets there first."

"As batters, players try to hit the ball out of reach of the fielding team and make a complete circuit around the bases for a 'home run'. The team that scores the most runs in nine innings—times at bat—wins the game."

"The key to winning is that you guys from Fantheon can probably hit a round ball with round bat more accurately than a human. For humans this can be quite difficult. As soon as tomorrow we can find out."

The Capital City Sports Stadium

A bus pulled to a stop in front of the stadium, and 15 large men in blue jeans and long-sleeved blue shirts and a similarly clad driver emerged and began walking up the ramp to the stadium floor.

Atlas, walking with Mr. Volt, remarked, "This may be the largest stadium in the world. It seats 150 thousand sports fans."

"Quite impressive," responded Volt.

Following Atlas, the group gathered around home plate. Atlas began distributing three boxes of gloves that the crew had brought in.

"Alright, ball players, come up and get your gloves. They go on the left hand."

Atlas walked up to home plate with a box of hardballs, pitched them up with his left hand a hit a few out to the field.

They seemed to have no problem fielding the balls. Atlas told the group that it was time for some real practice. He transferred a bat to one player and a box of balls to another. Without being told, the player with the baseballs moved to the pitcher's mound.

Speaking to the player with the bat, Atlas said "See if you can hit the ball, a so-called fly ball—that is, one that goes up and travels almost to the centerfield fence."

"Okay. Can Mr. Brass come up to the pitcher's mound? And we need a batter, how about how you, Mr. Copper? We will, of course, want everyone to try out each position."

The players were in place and Atlas was addressing Mr. Brass, the pitcher. "I assume you have seen the specs on the strike zone. What I would like to determine is just how accurately you can throw the ball. Let's start with a fastball at 100 miles an hour. What do you think, Mr. Brass?"

"Sir, we have all played a game somewhat like this. I believe that any of us can could hit this baseball bringing it up to around 100 miles per hour and hit any spot from here to the batter's strike zone within plus or minus one inch. Shall I proceed and find out? We might do plus or minus 1/4 inch at 50 miles per hour."

An infrared laser in his head was aimed precisely at the target spot. Brass stood motionless facing directly toward the batter. He uttered a quiet "Now", and his arm, which rested down at his side, rotated back from a position just under his shoulder at a remarkable speed and when straight up high, released the ball which would have hit the exact spot selected in the strike zone, except that Mr. Copper, at bat, swung and produced a perfect line drive. The ball hit the bottom of the centerfield fence, as was targeted.

During the rest of the day all the players tried this exercise. Atlas could not tell a single difference between any of them. They all executed the test goals perfectly.

The next day Atlas was telling the Secretary how it had gone. "Sir, the skill level of this group is amazing. I don't think there is any way one of our pro baseball teams could beat them. They could, if they wanted to, get 11 home runs with 11 batters in a row any time they wanted. On the other hand, they seem quite willing to dumb down to any level I suggest. They then could either win or lose depending on my wishes without a care either way. So, my suggestion is to go ahead with the plan of playing various pro teams and win some and lose some, giving the impression that this is indeed their level of skill. This should still make them popular and well known," said Atlas.

"All right. Let's go ahead. Perhaps it's better to have them come out as winners," said Secretary Russell.

Ten days later

The first game was billed as a free exhibition game between the local Capital City Tigers and the 15 androids who had recently arrived from Fantheon. No funny business. Just the absolute truth. The attendance was reasonable, about 50,000 mostly young people.

The androids emerged from the lower stadium in their new uniforms to light applause—looking almost human. The game proceeded without incident through eight innings without incident with the score tied at 8 to 8.

Atlas got them together in the dugout and said, "This has gone very well, guys, but now let's win! Pitch fast balls that hit the corners of the strike zone. Batters hit three home runs."

This yielded three struck out Tigers and three home runs with a final score of Tigers–8 to Astronauts–11.

Two of the home runs went completely over the stadium and down onto the parking lot where one of them went through the windshield of a school bus.

As the Tigers filed out of the stadium one player said to another in reference to the ninth inning, "Where in the hell did that come from?"

As the season progressed, interest in the Astronauts soared. They had played five games and lost only one, that one by just one point. It became clear to Atlas that winning yielded far more press and public notice than losing.

The Wrong Side of Capital City

The south end of Pearl Street in the downtown section of Capital City was not an attractive area. It consisted mainly of junk yards, abandoned buildings, construction equipment yards and seedy bars.

In the Moon Light Bar and Grill sat eight raggedy young men drinking draft beer. They were watching a baseball game on a big screen TV. But this was no ordinary game. They could hardly believe what was taking place before their eyes. Their favorite team, the Tigers, were not playing a normal team—they were playing a bunch of fucking robots. The young men had seen the robots before. How could they sit there and watch the inevitable ending? The robots will kick their asses all over the field and win the game. Pretty soon the Tigers were going to look like fools.

Bart Johnson could not take any more of this. He stood up and said, "How can our guys do this? Play against fucking robots! They are just about to make fools of themselves. In the ninth inning, we will look like idiots. My cousin Martha works downtown in the building planning department. You will not believe what she told me about the robots. They just flew in uninvited, about three months ago in their flying space contraptions. They're going to build a new museum downtown. And what do they charge? Nothing! They work for free," said Bart.

"Free? They charge nothing? Where do these guys stay at night?" asked Marley Rutherford.

"All 15 now stay in their flying machines out on the edge of town. But when they start construction, they claim they will work at the site 24 hours a day, seven days a week and never eat, never sleep, never take a shit. They don't need money. When they arrived, they took 900 pounds of gold to a bank."

"Unbelievable!" said Sid Lockhart.

"You got that right," said his brother Leon.

"If they succeed, you know what will happen. There will be more coming. You know it. We will all be out of business. My uncle Fletcher will be out of the oil business."

"No fucking way!" yelled Josh Grimes.

"Hey guys! We can't let this happen." said Rufus Rather.

Bart, standing and looking straight at his group said, "I propose we go get some sledge hammers from my uncle's warehouse, go to the stadium and when these assholes come out of the locker rooms after the game, we rearrange some robot body parts."

"Let's do it!" yelled Josh Grimes. "They ain't even alive. Who the fuck would care?"

They broke into a chant as the group marched out of the bar to their cars, "DO IT! DO IT! DO IT! DO IT!"

The Capital City Sports Stadium

The game had been over for about ten minutes and the fans were still filing out through the exits. In the Astronaut's locker room, the team did not shower, they simply took off their uniforms and donned their street clothes.

Atlas asked players Glass and Spark to help pick up the bats, balls and uniforms. The other players were leaving the room and walking back out onto the playing field.

Sid Lockhart, who had arrived earlier with binoculars, noted that Bart Johnson and his seven drinking buddies had borrowed his uncle's flatbed truck and two ladders. On a signal from his colleagues, the others had scampered up and over the back fence, weapons in hand, and were racing across the field towards the robots, yelling and whooping like wild Indians.

Volt looked over toward Brass and pointed as he said, "Who are they?" Brass replied, "I don't know, but they are coming straight at us. This looks like trouble."

Volt stepped forward to meet the first antagonist, who was yelling, "Hey, robot man, I'm gonna rearrange your fuckin' head."

He lifted a large sledge hammer up as high as he could. Just inches away, and already controlled by his threat electronics, Volt quickly grabbed the handle of the hammer from the attacker with his right hand and pushed the man to the ground with his left. Volt then leaped toward the man and put his foot on his chest, grabbed his left arm in both steel hands and wrenched it from his body at the shoulder joint. He held the severed arm in one hand and threw it up on into the fifth row of the stadium. A torrent of red blood gushed from the huge wound on the man's shoulder. He bled out so fast he never made a sound.

Josh Grimes was several feet to the left and somewhat ahead of his colleague and so focused on his own selected adversary that he was unaware that his friend Bart had already been destroyed by Mr. Volt.

"Hey there! Yeah, you with the leather face!"

"Yes?" replied Mr. Brass.

"You guys work for nothing for 24 hours a day. Right?"

Atlas and his two helpers had just walked out of the locker room and on to the field.

"What the fuck are the rest of us supposed to do? You know, the ones who are not fucking robots? Maybe it would be fairer if I put a little dent in that ugly face of yours?" At this he lifted up his hammer and lunged forward.

Mr. Brass, who had managed to wrest the short handled hammer from his antagonist, shoved it into his attacker's mouth and out the back side of his throat. With these horrific events in plain view, the other five young men from the Moon Light Bar and Grill took off running in a pell-mell frenzy back to their ladder, scrambled up and disappeared over the fence.

Atlas looked at Volt and the others and said, "This is not good, not good all. We need to get out of here immediately. The police will be here in minutes. Let's get on our bus and go. Now!"

In less than one minute all 15 players were in the bus. Atlas was close behind. He got in, jumped in the driver's seat and took off. They were only a few blocks away when they heard police sirens. Two police cars flew by them, unaware of who was in the bus. Twenty minutes later the players were pulling into the open field where they parked their Flyers.

Volt walked up to Atlas, who was still in the driver's seat, and said "Mr. Atlas, we want to thank you for all your help but it is clear this has not worked out. We are going to leave Theon."

Atlas leaned back and motioned toward the exit door. "Go."

"Perhaps we should go to Planet Earth. It's only 57 years away. No problem for us. We'd like to stay in touch though, best in private. The only way we can do that is if you keep one of our Flyers. What about at your house? Atlas sighed, and said "Yes, that's fine. We have a barn with large doors that could keep it hidden."

"Good," said Volt. " Here is what we can do. You and I take a Flyer and, moving up high so as not to be seen, go to your house and drop down silently and pull the machine into your barn. Then you take me in your car to the other Flyers. We need to get moving immediately."

"Okay. Let's go," said Atlas.

With the Flyer tucked in and the two ostensible beings almost ready to part, Atlas had to ask. "Mr. Volt, what went wrong? How could this have happened? I had no idea a bunch of low lifers would appear, seemingly out of nowhere, with no warning, and want to bash your heads in for taking a few construction jobs."

"I can think of only one possibility, Mr. Atlas. Perhaps they assumed that we were just the first wave of workers who would not need compensation.

Atlas responded, "But we thought Theon had received the gene modification therapy that calms down the well-known aggressive tendencies of Homo sapiens."

"If so, why wouldn't they contact some authorities or their newspaper, before coming down to the stadium to bash our heads in? Your friend Mother Nature has been talking about this for years," explained Volt.

"No, her gene therapy went to planet Earth. All our authorities thought we didn't need it."

Back Home

"Hello, dear. Sorry I missed dinner. I had a few problems to think about," slurred Atlas back at home.

"You are drunk!" said Mother Nature.

"Yes indeed, you got that right. But let me tell you something. You know that planet they call Theon? You know, the one we live on. That nice place, where unlike every other place, we have no problem with the aggressive nature of Homo sapiens? You wouldn't believe what I saw today in that nice place! Today," he gulped, "I witnessed two young very angry and very aggressive young men try to bash two sentient beings to death with sledge hammers!"

Mother Nature was stunned but quickly recovered her composure and said slowly, "Wait just a minute here. I know what we need. We need the GENE GUN."

Chapter Sixteen

More Steel

**Planet Earth
57 years later
Year 2082**

**Strategic Air Command Base
Bangor, Maine**

Major Tom McRenolds was gently knocking on the closed office door of the Base Commander, 64 year old Colonel Jones. The Major heard a deep voice say, "Come in." He opened the door and strolled into the office.

"Good morning, Major. Good to see you. Please sit down. What can I do for you?" said the Colonel.

"Well, sir, I am not sure how to explain it all. Let me start with some background. You may recall that many years ago a group at Patrick Air Force Base in Florida set up an automated system to scan outer space for any communications."

"Yeah, I remember that. Around 2030, I think. About 50 years ago."

"Yes sir, dead on. You have a sharp memory."

"Well, I was in high school then. And stories about the only alien we on Earth have ever encountered were still being told via books, movies, and TV shows. The public could not get enough. The son of a bitch had his camp no more than ten miles north of here in the woods," said the Colonel.

"Yes, Sir. I just looked it up. The android, they called him Mr. Steel, killed some people at a big meeting in Dallas in 2025. Cell phones recorded it all. But let me tell you what the Florida guys picked up just recently."

"Okay. Let's hear it".

"They picked up two roughly ten-minute conversations, both in languages never spoken on Earth. The first one they heard was probably from their ship to their home planet. The second was from their craft to here. In the first one, they heard two words in English: 'Steel' and 'Bangor'. The second communication contained the words: 'Steel' and 'Iceland'. The people in Florida heard all of the second conversation. The Florida guys used our Air Force Base in California on the second communication. Using triangulation they concluded that the ship was about 25,000 miles out and traveling about 600 mph. That should put them here in about 41 hours."

"Major, who else has heard this story?"

"The guys in Florida said they briefed the Secretary of Defense first and then called me. They advised me to tell no one else but you."

"Excellent." The Colonel rose from his chair, opened his office door and asked his secretary to see if she could set up a secure phone call to Secretary Summers in Washington.

The call was placed and the Colonel summarized, "They are probably going to Iceland to pick up Steel. Do we really care what happens to Steel?" He listened to Summer's response and then confirmed, " Yes, it would be excellent PR to capture Steel."

Just then Summers said, "Hold on. I have a message from Florida coming in. Hold on…Coming in…just…a minute."

After a tense ten minute wait, the Colonel explained to McRenolds that four spacecraft, carrying human-size androids, wanted to land in an open space near Washington, D.C. and see the President, at his convenience. They were coming from a planet called Theon, which they claimed was four light years from Earth.

"Here is word-for-word what they said," the Colonel said. "Let me read it out loud to you." He then read the text message Secretary Summers had just sent.

"We have been traveling for 57 years. We have valuable gifts for the United States and are not coming to cause any trouble. Two members of the crew would like to see the President at any time at his convenience. We would be pleased to deliver a more formal presentation if preferred. Please pick up the two of us with armed police or military when ready, if that makes you feel safer. This same group may come to our landing site when ready to schedule our meeting.

Mr. Volt
Six days later at the White House

Volt and Brass were in a large conference room at the White House. About half the people in the room were seated in front of a stage in a small theater. The first two rows were occupied by the President and his Cabinet and other government officials. Others were gradually seating themselves.

Behind the seating was an open area with a bar where coffee and pastries were being served. Two women with video recorders were moving around. Four armed men in police uniforms also stood near the side walls. Two of the policemen held large weapons openly at their sides. About 50 people were present.

Secretary Summers rose from his seat next to the President and walked to a microphone set up in front of the audience.

"Everyone please take your seats. As everyone knows—last Monday, July 12, four spacecraft arrived carrying 15 androids. The spacecraft are now housed in two barns just outside the city limits. No one should try to find them. At this time we will not tolerate any attempts to see or interview the crew. Mr. Volt, you may begin."

Volt, who had been standing against the conference room wall next to the armed policeman, moved over to the microphone. He was dressed in a baseball uniform. His voice was that of a human male, essentially identical in tone to that of actor Morgan Freeman.

"Good morning, President Harris. My name is Volt. I have one colleague with me here today. His name is Mr. Brass."

Brass stood and spoke in a voice identical to that of Liam Neeson. "Good morning, sir. I am truly honored to see your cabinet members here as well. I have met some of them already. Good morning, Secretary Summers. Good morning, Colonel Jones."

The group murmured, "Good morning."

Volt continued, "Why are we here? Well, we are here to give you something of great value. And why would do that? We want to be surrounded by goodwill. Surrounded by beings who like us. We seek everlasting goodwill. It is unthinkable to us to cause you harm. Our home planet is called Fantheon. It is about 15 light years away from here. That means light or radio signals would travel at their normal speed of 186,000 miles per second in 15 years. Solid objects cannot travel at such speeds, of course. But after many years of working on the problem, we have been able to transport solid objects, like ourselves, at 7% of the speed of light. Humans cannot tolerate such speeds. In any case, it took 214 years for the 15 of us to travel from Fantheon to Theon. It would take a human over 2,000 years. That is completely unworkable, of course. It took us 57 years to arrive here from Theon, which is only four light years distant. By the way, sir, please feel free to interrupt me at any time if something is not clear."

The President asked, "Why are you in baseball uniforms?" and a brief ripple of chatter went through the audience.

"Excellent question, sir. This is our second stop after leaving our home, Planet Fantheon. As I just mentioned, our first stop was at planet Theon. We were planning on constructing a museum in their capital city. It was to be a gift from Fantheon. Construction is our primary expertise. I will explain this in more detail later, if that is alright. But it was thought by the Theon people that the first thing we should do was to become better known and accepted by the general population of Theon. It was suggested that playing baseball would accomplish this. My understanding is the game is played here as well and that indeed it originated here. We became quite skilled at playing the game. So, we have a proposition for you. Arrange three games with one of your most successful professional teams. The games must be played in one of your professional stadiums and TV broadcasted in the usual manner. If we do not win all three games, we will give the team 900 pounds of gold. Also, we would like to deposit the gold into one of your local banks as soon as possible."

"In playing the game we will adjust our behavior such that your team players will not be injured by us. For example, we will not throw a baseball faster than 100 mph unless you give us permission. We will not slide into any bases. We will not attempt to steal any bases."

The president replied, "Mr. Volt, that sounds very intriguing. Please see me tomorrow at one o'clock to discuss this idea."

"Yes, sir. I'll be there. May I also bring Mr. Brass?"

"Of course."

"Okay. Let me continue. One goal I have set for myself is to be completely transparent. There are some negatives to reveal. First. I have a quantity of radioactive plutonium in my chest. I may be too dangerous to be close to. Let's find out. Mr. Brass, would you please bring up the Geiger counter we've borrowed. Switch it on, please." Brass did as instructed. "You can hear the ticking sound of background radiation. This is now at a perfectly normal level. Now please bring it in close and move it around and see if you can find high radiation spots."

Brass did as instructed. "Nothing. Maybe there really is no radioactive material in there." said Brass.

"Just batteries. Brass, here is a key to a small door on my back. Please open it just a crack."

Brass opened the small door on Volt's back. A sudden roar sounded from the Geiger counter. Brass slammed the opening shut. He relocked it and handed Volt the key.

"That's a good reason to keep one's back door locked!"

Gentle laugher rose from the audience.

"Hey Brass. I actually told a joke. My first." Brass, with a scowl, replied, "Very impressive."

More laughter.

But seriously, gentlemen and ladies, a highly contaminated region could develop which could extend for blocks and be difficult to clean up. The half-life of plutonium 239 is 24,000 years.

"Let's next turn to another subject. When we landed in Theon back in 2025 our welcome came apart well before a year had passed. Mr. Steel, now in hiding, eventually experienced something similar, after having been here in full disguise for 150 years."

"Here is the reason. Our makers, our designers, back in Fantheon decided to include a certain hardwired feature, for our own self-preservation. If threatened—really threatened, not by mere shouted insults, or even verbal threats. Not just rants but people actually using weapons such as guns, sledge hammers, swords and the like. If a gun has fired, or a hammer is in motion in the next few milliseconds our normal brain is turned off and we go into an attack mode. Higher speed circuits are activated and our power supply goes jet-engine. We instantly dismember our adversaries so fast that it's a blur to anyone watching. If we happen to be in a crowd, cell phones would record this. Some phones would angle upward and catch body parts flying in the air. Perfect for the 6:00 P.M. TV news horror show! But in one minute or less, alternative high speed electronics are turned off. We look around at the mayhem, yet can remember none of it. The various onlookers, if any are still close, would be in panic, running away toward the exits as fast as they could. This is more or less what happened back in 2015 in Dallas, Texas with Mr. Steel."

"We believe this self-defense circuit can be turned off. If we do further business here, we will turn it off. It should be turned off! We will let you do tests to make sure. Unlike we 15, Mr. Steel was fabricated in Theon, following detailed instructions from Fantheon who had already established high-speed communications between the two planets. Steel had established a relationship with a well-known technical genius and inventor Dr. Robert Mann. The full story is going to take some time." Volt paused. "President Harris, I have been speaking for some time. Perhaps you would like to take a break. I notice you have quite a number of your people tied up here."

"No. Mr. Volt, let's finish the story about Mr. Steel. Then we can break for one hour. That should take us to around 1:00 P.M. We can then decide how to proceed. Please, continue."

"Yes, sir. As I was about to say, Dr. Mann was on a camping trip by himself in one of the densely wooded park areas above Banger. As it turned out, Mann had inadvertently planned to camp quite close to Steel's secret hiding place. Steel had excavated a large cave inside the foot of a mountain where he had set up a secret residence."

"Let me explain why Steel came to planet Earth in the first place. On this subject I can only tell you what I have picked up during the several communications we had picked up, Flyer to Flyer, as we made our way across 4 times 10 to the 13th miles of nothingness. There were three factors at work."

"Firstly, certain people on Fantheon were simply anxious to learn more about planet Earth. Secondly, they wished to continue their practice of transferring extremely advanced technical information capabilities to other worlds. Scientists on Theon state that Fantheon is one million years ahead of them in science and technology, and they themselves are 150 years ahead of Earth."

"The third factor is more controversial. For many centuries archeologists on both Fantheon and Theon have discussed evidence that shows that the human species Homo sapiens are too aggressive to survive for long. Eventually they will destroy themselves in a country-against-county all-out nuclear war. Two solutions to the problem have been considered. One, a world government could be established, where all countries of a planet become, in effect, states. This would be followed by total disarmament. The second solution to the problem includes disarmament and gene editing toward a reduction of the property of aggressiveness in Homo sapiens."

"In the field of gene editing, it is my understanding that scientists both in Fantheon and Theon had been working for many years on a gene modification method that could be easily delivered in one dose. Since the human populations of Fantheon are not Homo sapiens and Theon had already gone to the alternative solution, the only place left to try it out was Earth. That was exactly what happened. Steel was assembled in Theon according to the detailed instructions from Fantheon. The gene modifying materials were assembled by a woman whom I think was called Mary Nature, a famous geneticist there. I'm not sure about the name, but in any case, she provided the gene doses. Steel was transported to Earth. The voyage to Earth took 100 years. So, he arrived here in 1910. I also heard the program went well and Steel was supervised by the Ms. Nature for the next 100 years. How that was possible, I cannot say."

Secretary Summers, who had been squirming in his chair for the past half hour, stood and said in a rather hostile tone, "Mr. Volt, I've been quiet and I have not interrupted you, but what the fuck is going on here? You say you arrived from Theon and were made in Fan-something. Our astronomers have never heard of such places. I doubt they even exist. You are telling us that we are so dumb they had to send a robot over to fix us! A really smart one like you, right?"

With a red face he continued, "You want us to replace electric power generation equipment with a plutonium gadget? Do you realize how long it took to go solar, wind and safe nuclear? A process which consumed trillions of dollars? And 35 agonizing years. But we did it. All over the world. And now are we finally seeing temperatures lowering. You think we are going to shut down solar and go with a new technology? Never. Not in a million years."

He took a big breath and practically yelled, "And the final insult. We are so fucking dumb that your buddies at this planet Theon, that we've never heard of, decided we were going to nuke everyone. So, they put this robot together and sent him here to fix our screwed-up genes. Tell me, Mr. Volt, just where is this famous Mr. Steel?"

"I don't know exactly," replied Volt.

"Okay, where is he approximately?" said Summers.

"Under the present circumstances, which now seem to have suddenly turned very negative, it would be unethical for me to tell you."

"Negative, huh? You haven't seen negative. Sheriff! Arrest the two robots or whatever the fuck they are."

Brass grabbed the video camera away from the filmmaker, who was just a few steps from him, looked at Volt and said, "Magnet," and quickly moved towards a large window. Volt nodded and headed in the same direction.

The sheriff aimed his weapon and yelled "Stop or I will shoot!

Both electric men turned towards the sheriff and simultaneously struck their chests very hard with their left hands. A magnetic field of immense strength vectored out from the two electric men, slamming them both against either side of the window. In order to prevent injury to themselves, in two seconds both electric men dropped to the floor.

Anything of steel not firmly held or embedded, such as nails and screws, was ripped from hands, pockets, and off of clothing. A horizontal hailstorm of steel ensued, loaded mainly with guns and knives, and streaked across the room headed for the window. Guns struck the wall around the window with a boom and some smashed through the glass and landed on the lawn outside. Volt stood and turned facing the window, when through a small metal barrel which had whirled out from high on his chest, jets issued a glowing liquid stream. The liquid swelled and ignited blue-white, blew out the remaining glass, and melted a hole some five feet in diameter in the wall. The two electric men, now up on their feet, backed up about ten feet and ran toward the opening, diving through it and onto the grass. They were immediately on their feet again and running at 60 miles per hour towards an eight-foot-tall fence, which they effortlessly leapt over. It took them two seconds from house to fence.

By the time the White House guards realized someone was running from the building and they had leveled up their weapons to target them, they were gone.

The remaining 13 electric men, who had been listening to the White House meeting via a transmission from Volt, had quietly and nonviolently subdued their guards and brought the Flyers out of the garages.

Volt and Brass raced up to their Flyers with their bodies dangerously nearing a high temperature overload. Their colleagues removed their baseball uniforms and threw several pails of water on them, producing steam, which rose in a white cloud.

Flying Away

Still wet, they immediately went aboard their Flyers and took off, climbing upward to about 40,000 feet. Volt suggested they go north near Iceland. "We need to collect Steel, but they may be already in wait for just such a meeting." They all headed north toward Norway.

"Well," said Volt, "we just blew our second attempt to help prevent Homo sapiens from destroying themselves in an all-out nuclear war. Now we know at least which country is likely to start it."

"Could be. But I thought it was simpler than that. Summers simply did not want to be shown a better way to generate electricity than solar and wind—his baby," said Brass.

"As it turned out, I had a suspicion that the United States was so proud of itself that it would not take our technology and run with it. So, using their internet, which was very well done, I have considered and studied other countries that might be more responsive. In terms of economic need, we have the whole continent of Africa which has 53 countries where virtually none of them enjoy a strong economy."

"How can that be?" asked Volt.

"I haven't found anyone who knows, but I think it might be that they still embrace their many hundreds of separate tribes, each of which spoke a separate language, wanted to live only in a specific area, dressed in a certain fashion, ate only certain foods, and so on. Persuading all these people to work happily together in one factory may be impossible."

"I bet you are right," said Volt.

"For example, Nigeria, which produces lots of cement requiring lots of energy, speaks over 500 languages. Another product requiring lots of electricity is aluminum and it is also produced in Africa. Aluminum originates from bauxite, an ore found in Guinea, Mozambique and Ghana. Guinea is the largest producer. At least 43 languages are spoken in Mozambique. Ghana is also a multilingual country with over 80 ethnic languages that are spoken nowhere else. English is Ghana's official foreign language but this may be problematic because of the country's history of colonization, a period about which many justifiably harbor bitter feelings."

"I don't think Africa will work for us." said Volt.

"I agree, said Brass. "How about this? We look at countries that still use some nuclear power plants, have stable well-performing economies, and are well educated in the Sciences. This would include Australia, South Korea, Great Britain, Germany, France, Japan, Holland and China, among others. Once running well, these counties could spread the technology to the rest of the world."

"When we enter a country, we should send in three of us at a time. The others should be nearby in the Flyers, as before, for backup if needed."

"We need to pick up Steel first and see what he says." Bass reminded them.

Steel was picked up near Norway's coastal city of Stavanga. He, of course, was very pleased to be rescued. He liked the plan Brass proposed. Embittered about how he had been pursued as a crazed murdering machine, he suggested they stay away from the U.S.

By the time they were ready to see China, seven years had passed and the 15 electric men were world-famous. Today, their four Flyers were being carried in massive flatbed trucks down the streets of China's Capital City, Beijing, where a huge parade was underway in their honor. Using U235, the new electricity generation devices were already nearing production. All the Chinese really wanted now was help in building the high speed planet-to-planet communication equipment. Detailed information about the new electricity generation technology had been on the Internet for the past five years.

Reducing Diseases

Thus far, in numerous talks with Mother Nature the world had already eliminated several diseases from Planet Earth including Alzheimer's, Parkinson's, and Diabetes. Others were on their way out as well. Next to go would be cancer.

Green Electric Power

The plutonium electric power generation device was an enormous success around the world, except in the United States where the technical community still insisted the process was not competitive. It is true that plutonium set into fission by neutron bombardment could generate heat energy equivalent to the total amount of energy in the US by converting only 500 pounds of plutonium. But then this had to be converted to electric power. Some E-power generation efficiencies may be compared to better understand the position of the U.S.

1. Today's nuclear power plants, depending where they operate, as a percent of total capacity: 30 to 90%.

2. Natural gas turbine 38%.
3. Thermo electric pn device maximum 20%
4. Hydroelectric—Input power has no cost.
5. Solar PV electric—Input power has no cost.
6. Wind turbine—Input power has no cost.

New Homo Sapiens Create a Paradise on Earth

Did Homo sapiens eventually destroy themselves in a nuclear holocaust? No, they didn't. After about 250 years following the gene implants in the US, about half of the U.S. population had become less aggressive. In another 250 years the new genes had calmed down half the world. They were dominant genes and the whole world eventfully forgot about war and completely disarmed itself.

There were no ICBMs, no missiles, no wars, no guns, no weapons, no bullets, no murders, no electric chairs, no lethal injections, no armies, no tanks, no battle ships, no atomic bombs, no submarines, no bombs, no navies, no air force, no generals, no arrests, no admirals, no FBI, no wardens, no police chiefs, no sectaries of defense, no criminals, no sheriffs, no violence, no pollution, no police, no robberies, no jails, no prisons. The world population dropped in half to become four billon and then leveled off. How did they accomplish that? It was obvious to all that birth rates had to be reduced. So they were.

The world's vast forests returned.

Finally, how many android men eventually stood on planet Earth? 500. And how many on planet Fantheon, with their one-million-year technical lead?

Who Knows? Maybe Atlas.

A Few Words From the Author

I realize that writing this last part is rarely if ever done. Sorry, I had to do it. What did you think about the last few lines in the book? I must mention this. The ending. The glorious ending. Indeed. I wrote this whole spooky story so I could write the last 250 words. To me it's a positive, super wonderful ending. No more wars. Ever. No crime. No prisons. No pollution. No police. No suffering. No more lies. Just the right number of people a planet like Earth could sustain for many tens of thousands of years. But could such a thing really happen? Of course you already know the answer. Do you think people would go for gene editing? Many do not even trust the government to give them vaccinations. Oh well, we can dream.

The End